Memorial. I am delighted by a mole and a sparrow, who face objections to their marriage. I cheer for a child inspired by her grandfather, enthralled by young men involved in war, and excited by clever people overcoming challenges. This is a book you will want to buy, relish, and keep on your shelf for frequent re-reading."

—**Betty Wood**, Eugene, Oregon, member, Creative Writing Group: Osher Lifelong Learning Institute, University of Oregon

Praise for *Meanderings of a Bent Mind*

"The stories in *Meanderings of a Bent Mind* are absolutely wonderful...Not only do the individual stories resonate with insight and imagery, but there's also a profound gentleness that runs throughout...like a thread that ties everything together. This is the kind of book everyone should have at the ready. An explorative and exciting (yet calming) set of quick reads that dare to stretch the imagination and venture into uncertain territory."

—**Livvie Taylor-Young**, Eugene, Oregon, facilitator, Creative Writing Group: Osher Lifelong Learning Institute, University of Oregon

"Immerse yourself in lovely tales of real and imaginative characters in vivid environments as they explore and discover friendship and connections only the heart comprehends."

—**Lorene Lederer**, San Carlos, California, member, Creative Writing Group: Osher Lifelong Learning Institute, University of Oregon

"These stories, wisps of plot and character really, speak to a sense of innocence and wonder that for many adults has long since disappeared. They fit well with a child's fleeting sensibilities, and a grown-up's fleeting memories."

—**Randall C. Luce**, Eugene, Oregon member, Creative Writing Group: Osher Lifelong Learning Institute, University of Oregon

"I very much enjoyed *Meanderings of a Bent Mind*, Gordon Nagai's latest publication in what has become a diverse body of work. This beautiful collection of short stories offers the reader a variety of plots and settings, from deep green forests to the far reaches of outer space.

Mr. Nagai is adept at the art of the short story, delivering whole new worlds in deceptively compact forms. The author has a way of describing scenes that put the reader directly into the mind of his characters and their already-unfolding action.

Written with a gentle, wry humor, these stories of strong, resourceful young people often end in satisfying ways as the bad guys lose and the young people once again outwit their foes.

Charming and gentle, I found myself picking up this collection before bed, a way to calm my mind after long and troubling days. I hope you find the journey through his stories as enjoyable as I did."

—**Alice Kirby**, Redmond, Oregon, member,
Creative Writing Group: Osher Lifelong Learning Institute,
University of Oregon

"Gordon Nagai has used his incredible imagination to write a book that captivates readers of all ages. *Meanderings of a Bent Mind* is filled with fascinating and divergent short stories, inhabited by interesting characters, painted with brilliant settings, and provoking unexpected emotions.

Each story is a different experience. There are wonderful, anthropomorphized animals, stories about young children and what they learn from and about their parents, grandparents, other adults, and authority figures. There are fairy tales with deep meanings, tales of heroism, and many tales of wisdom.

Characters often find themselves transported to sites of historical events, outer space, secret hiding places, wild country, Arctic cold, desert heat, space stations, and magical kingdoms.

Gordon grabs our feelings. I am deeply moved when a child's best friend dies, and another child 'meets' her father at the Vietnam

MEANDERINGS *of a* BENT MIND

MEANDERINGS of a BENT MIND

The Journeys of an Introvert

GORDON HIDEAKI NAGAI

M·P·P
www.MissionPointPress.com

Published by Mission Point Press

2554 Chandler Rd.
Traverse City, MI 49696
(231) 421-9513
MissionPointPress.com

Softcover ISBN: 978-1-965278-75-8
Library of Congress Control Number: 2025910379

Printed in the United States of America

For Barbara Nagai—my best friend and lifelong partner
for sixty-four years...

Contents

Introduction

"A Fable is something that in the telling you have the sense it did happen sometime in your childhood..."

—Anon.

We are a people of stories—short stories, epic stories, stories with a shadow of mystery, stories that take your breath away or make you misty-eyed. For eons we passed stories along from father to son, grandfather to granddaughter, around campfires at night. Those elders who knew the older times were our storytellers.

We learned our history as a people through these stories. They were simple and homespun, yet they were profound, for they helped define who we were, taught us how we thought and what we believed.

We continue to be a people of stories. Our world is so much more complex today than in our past, not least of which is the pace of change.

For our ancient ancestors it took days and even weeks to notice the days were getting shorter. Now we know this storm is expected to blow over by morning.

Despite the complexity and speed of our world today, stories remain central to who we are and what we are about.

Computers are ubiquitous in our world. They are at once masterful and necessary aids in our daily lives, and dastardly overbearing villains that cause us no end of misery. It's a sort of love-hate relationship.

But at the end of the day, after we've shut down the computer and put aside the cares of the world, when the strains of the fast-paced mach-five vibrations settle to nil, we can curl up with a story of our choosing and enter that netherworld of make-believe that soothes the savage breast and eases the bounds of time.

There we meet wizards and shamans, and all manner of friends from our journey—this from our own personal and intimate story, and from our story as a people.

I'd like to think the stories herein are my personal stories. I believe they are. But they are more—they came not just from a source within tempered by the inner fires of my personal journey, they emerged as easily from the wellspring of memory traces of the race, from the cauldron at the heart of a people.

Each of our lives is a story, and to live our life as a story sometimes is easier done than said. We tell stories because it gives us life in the telling. More importantly, we tell stories because we can do no other...

Reason and wonder why...

Prologue

Childhood is a precious and wonder-filled time. Our experience of it was fresh and unfettered by the whims of the mind, and we were able to launch ourselves into the realms of daydreams, make-believe, and fantasy.

The short stories I present in *Meanderings* are a window into the past of my childhood, memory traces of wonder-filled times in a land of Merlin and unicorns and knights in shining armor.

When I was a child, the pace of life, even in the larger cities, was slower than today's craziness. Where I grew up there were fields and orchards to walk barefoot in, feeling the cool earth between my toes; barbed-wire fences placed there to divide and protect, but which were challenges to climb through, hoping you wouldn't get caught on the upper strand; fields of alfalfa you could run hell-bent through, and once spent fall down in with your face to the cerulean skies and feel the pain of the air entering and exiting your lungs.

And on those mornings when the farmer mowed his field you were drenched in the aroma of freshly mown alfalfa, and there's nothing in the world that matches or betters that smell.

There was Mrs. Taylor, fourth grade, a motherly type who taught me the power of books; and Mr. Kirby, my fifth-grade teacher who planted the seeds of music in my heart.

There were those games of marbles in big circles drawn in the dirt in a time when school playgrounds were allowed to have yards without macadam. There I am knuckling down with my favorite periwinkle in my hands, with the admonition of the principal ringing in my ears not to play for keeps under the penalty of some terrible punishment.

There were those restless summer nights under a thin sheet awaiting sleep to overtake me, listening to the wail of a steam engine in the distant darkness, and those early pre-dawn mornings lying in bed, looking out through the east-facing window waiting for the sky to light up from the atom bomb tests in the Nevada desert.

When we are stretched beyond our reach by life's happenings, we often are tempted to pull out all the stops and, in the process, grasp at measures that in our more serene, collected moments we wouldn't choose because they go against our own self-interests.

In those times especially it behooves us to reach down deep within and instead bring out gems from our past, lessons learned and answers that heal.

Then is the time to remember rightly, because it's a matter of survival. In the face of such important choices, there is something to be said for nostalgia as a good thing, especially about things from our childhood.

Nostalgia is funny that way—it colors our remembrances with a fuzzy glow, so we have to look hard sometimes for the reality in it all.

When events and people are seen through the soft-focus lens of hindsight it gives them a kinder edge, smooths out some of the wrinkles, and tempers the sometimes-harsh view we hold of those experiences, of certain people, and of ourselves.

This doesn't mean holding on to unreality or anything false, but to retain the best even in the worst of our experiences and the worst of the people who may have wronged us.

Not a simple task, but worth it if we can muster that as our response.

Many of our childhood memory traces sport elements that can serve the function of healing wounds.

There is an ancient proverb that goes something like this: Carry forward the flame from the altar of the past but leave the ashes. That's a good lesson for all of life.

Willows in the Wind

Renee crouched behind the fence and watched in silence as the rest of her family arrived at the church. It was mid-morning, and the chill of winter was gone, replaced by the growing warmth of spring.

The sun played hide-and-seek amid scattered clouds, giving the day alternately a subdued and moody cast among some spots of brightness. This was most appropriate as far as Renee was concerned, except the bright spots didn't suit her mood.

Earlier in the week, she had overheard her parents talking about the tragedy, and ran out of the house, tears streaming down her face, slamming the back door in anger.

Charlie Winslow had died because of a freak occurrence no one could explain in words that made sense to Renee. His funeral was today, and Renee wasn't handling it very well at all.

Charlie was one of those rare spirits who grace the earth from time to time, leaving a telltale mark on all those whose paths they've crossed. He made a connection with Renee from their first contact, and they were immediate and fast friends. He had a sense of humor that was outrageous, and a smile and a twinkle in his eyes that touched your heart and usually made for a better day.

Charlie was definitely an old soul, and Renee and her family were touched by that and welcomed him in as though he were family.

He and Renee often went to their secret cave, spending days in such secrecy as only children entertain. Actually, everyone knew where this secret spot was, it being one of those places only hidden amid shadows in the mind of a child. All Charlie and Renee knew was that pirates and buccaneers and all manner of marauding types never came around this special place—of course they didn't, it was secret.

Their hideaway was a minor indentation, hardly a cave at all, carved in a hillside by ancient forces of nature, obscured now in the midst of a stand of black oak trees and set back not far from the old dirt road to Crystal Lake.

Everyone knew that when you didn't see Charlie or Renee on any given day they were most likely out at their "secret hiding place." Everyone smiled and winked an eye over it.

Charlie was nearly twelve, and a very old twelve years of age at that. His parents were archaeologists of some renown, and he and his family had lived in some of the most exotic places on earth—places with strange-sounding names to a New Englander, but which Charlie took in stride as pretty much normal, at least for him and his family.

∾   ∾   ∾

Recently, a little over a month ago, his parents (to the excitement of locals) undertook a most promising excavation at Charleston Sound just north of Beaverton on the coast, a location thought to be a ceremonial site for indigenous peoples dating back to the period of the early 900s BCE. Beaverton was a sleepy little place that seemed to have remained unchanged since that time.

The ebb of time was as molasses in January. Everything in town closed on Saturdays and Sundays, and families did things together as families—quaint, and a throwback to another time.

Charlie loved these times with family, especially his little sister, Ariel, who was a very old two going on seventeen. Ariel doted on Charlie and would have tagged along with him like a leech, except their parents knew enough to ensure a little privacy for him.

Charlie, though, seemed to take it all in stride, spending considerable time by choice with her, reading her stories, taking her for walks, and sometimes just sitting with her as she dozed off into afternoon slumber. Family was very important to Charlie, and he didn't mind his sister as a tagalong.

The day Renee first met Charlie there was something magical in the air. She had just left the 10 o'clock church service at the corner of Leavenworth and Downing Streets and was racing with the wind blowing through her hair, her shirttail now pulled out and flying behind.

As she rounded the corner of the alley behind Stuckey's hardware, she caught movement out of the corner of her eye and deftly sidestepped a shadowy figure walking in the other direction. She skidded to a stop, sand pebbles scraping under the rubber soles of her sneakers—and there he was.

He was tall and slender, his shock of auburn hair standing out like a beacon in the sunlight. His eyes were hazel-green and penetrated you with such intensity that you felt almost intruded upon,

except you sensed he had only the most harmless of intentions—
you were safe with Charlie. You could tell that right off, as he was
fair transparent from the first contact.

"Hi," he said, grinning. "Great move."

"Thanks."

"Great brakes, too."

"Yeah—do that a lot—need that a lot," she countered, the beginnings of a smile moving across her lips.

"What's your name?"

"Renee. You?"

"Charlie. Wanna go over to the sound and throw rocks into the
water?"

"Now?"

"Yep."

"Sure." And they were off and running with the wind at their
backs, their eyes bright and broad grins lighting up their faces.

⊰ ⊰ ⊰

Charlie's parents were originally from California. Moreover, they
were from Northern California and the San Francisco Bay Area,
which put them pretty far to the left of most of middle-America. So
much so that they were at best oddities in the conservative confines
of Beaverton, and at worst the objects of much negative projection
as the bearers of evil to this quaint seacoast town.

Evil is as evil does—for some in town Charlie's parents were a
most distressing presence, with their liberal West Coast way of
thinking. In a small town differing loyalties stand stark and severe
in the light of day, and often take on a dark cast in the midst of
twilight shadows.

Most people were civil to Charlie's parents, cordial and courte-
ous as bespoke good breeding, but not close. And in difficult times,

8

that distance could become a yawning abyss of immense inner space, or more to the point, prejudice. Charlie, though, always thought of it as a spur to the possibility of meeting new people.

≈   ≈   ≈

The day before the tragedy, Charlie and Renee had gone to their cave to read comics and spend time together.

The day was just like any other for the two—a mix of talk spaced with silences as deep as the sky was high. In those silences they read a favorite comic book or lay on their stomachs watching the scurrying of ants around their hills, or just listened to the wind rustling the leaves of the trees above as they daydreamed dreams of whatever.

When they talked in quiet tones they touched on everything, including school, nature, what they thought about brothers and sisters, remembering steam engines coming in down at the train station, and Renee's budding interest in science, especially astronomy.

Now, Charlie knew a lot about a lot of things, science included, and when he talked about what happened in the night skies it brought chills to Renee.

Time seemed to stand still within the confines of their secret cave, its boundaries blown out to the edges of their imaginations, transporting them beyond the outer reaches of even their own personal galaxy.

Charlie was perfectly at home in these transportations, and relished them—no, make that he loved them. Renee, being a really good sport, gladly went along for the ride; to Charlie, she was the only one who could equal him on his mind walks through wonder-filled galaxies. They were a perfect match.

≥   ≥   ≥

Then, a strange darkness crept into the corners of their world. At first it was only an uneasiness felt below the levels of awareness, but it gradually grew, becoming a presence in their minds.

A change was taking place in their intimate world, and change is always fraught with the unknown.

Ah, youth—life is eternal, never-ending, and a joy and a challenge, and change is nothing if only something different.

"Get out! Go away!" uttered Renee, her arms thrust skyward, her index fingers pointing toward the zenith, her hazel eyes ablaze, reflecting a deep resolve within.

"Be gone!" muttered Charlie. "Gone ... Ixnay!" And he, too, thrust his arms toward the heavens, his right hand balled into a fist, his left clutching a Marvel Comic.

Renee screamed; Charlie shouted.

Renee responded from deep within. She closed her eyes and threw back her head, her hair flying.

Charlie pushed back, his two hands fending off the darkness in the corners of his mind now projected above the ether. And the two fell into a heap, exhausted, their arms and legs spent, their minds bent from the fray, but laughing so hard their stomachs ached.

Season's greetings, change—the season is summer, and summer is forever. "Hoo-Hah...!"

≥   ≥   ≥

Death came unannounced in the wee hours of Thursday morning. It neither knocked, nor gave cause—there were no warning signs, no indications that anything was wrong, nothing to cause alarm or indicate that anything was anything but fine.

It came as pressures blew out a weak spot in the main artery feeding the brain, an internal explosion that ripped into the cranial cavity, spilling precious lifeblood until the pressure there was too great. It was all but over in mere seconds.

Death came with sharp pains that were wrenching to the mind, causing all thought to fly in the face of dread if only briefly, leaving the breath of life ebbing, just ebbing, until the stillness and darkness merged as one.

Then, all was quiet, the undercurrent of one heartbeat silenced forever. Charlie was dead at age eleven, going on a very mature twelve.

Renee could not believe it—would not believe it. It just wasn't fair!

"Who does he think he is doing this, dammit?" swore Renee aloud. "Charlie, you get your ass back down here!" she flung at the heavens.

She half expected to see him walk in her front door any moment to tell her it was all a very bad joke.

Her parents were as devastated as Renee, and tried to comfort her through all of this, but Renee was deeply hurt, enraged and disbelieving, and had a difficult time accepting any reassurances and support.

Who could have known? How could this have happened? Why didn't someone do something for Charlie?

Renee pushed the weeds aside and peered between the boards of the fence next to the sanctuary. The church organ sounded behind the stained-glass windows above her, melancholy and distant and lost to the heavens—there was only the pain, and it wouldn't go away.

Tears came and went, and came and went away again, leaving her eyes misty and red-rimmed. But the pain in her chest wouldn't leave her.

The music stopped, and Renee could hear the muffled voice of the pastor. She couldn't make out his words, but his voice was soothing, likely voicing the pain of wonder lost and invoking the powers of some higher plane to give solace to the heart in distress. He would touch on the appreciation and debt felt by the townspeople for having known Charlie, if only for a blink in the span of time he was here.

The murmured eulogy continued, and Renee sat in silence, a gentle breeze wafting through her space in the sun.

"A nickel for your thoughts," came a voice from behind her. She turned and found her dad standing there, his hand resting on the top of the fence.

"I'm sorry I got so mad the other day, Dad," she whispered.

"I know, Hon," he replied. "He was something else, that Charlie, and it hurts that he's gone."

"Why, Dad? Why does it hurt so much?"

Dad didn't answer right away, but knelt and sat in the grass beside her next to the fence. "It hurts anytime someone leaves us." Silence.

"Charlie was a good friend, and anytime something good is gone, it matters."

Again, silence. "Will the hurting stop?" she asked at last.

"No, not all of it—but in time some of it will heal. You'll remember Charlie and the good things you and he shared, though you'll continue to feel the loss. Then one day you'll just be thankful that he came your way."

Dad sat in silence and laid his arm across Renee's shoulder, pulling her to him.

"I love that he came by and I got to know him, Dad," whispered Renee, tearing up.

"Me too, Hon..."

Ghost Riders of the Mist

Jason sat under the swinging sign in front of the old hotel. His daughter Colleen had gone back inside to the gift shop to buy a postcard for her mom, and because of the stifling heat Jason had elected to wait outside.

Sitting in the shade gave the illusion that it was cooler, though he knew it wasn't really.

Colleen was an energetic ten-year-old in love with the old west, and a precocious student of Native American Peoples. This vacation was in part for her.

It had been an uneventful trip thus far; they were on their way to meet her mother Phyll in Carlsbad, New Mexico, where she had been the featured lecturer at the annual convention of NASA, the North American Society of the Antiquities.

⋟　　⋟　　⋟

Phyll was Dr. Phyllis Barnum, wife and mother, archaeologist, professor and lecturer, author of the recent bestseller *Digging for Fun and Prophet*, a scholarly though readable accounting of her study of the sages and medicine men of the Navajo.

Her parents were both professors, though her father as an electrical engineer was in a field on the far side of Phyll's interests and predilections.

Her mother was an English professor, with a decided preference for latter-day poets of Eastern Europe. Her facility with the English language she passed on to Phyll in her ease and ability with communications, both in the spoken as well as written word. Words represented power, and Phyll was masterful in their use.

There were a lot of things about Phyll one could easily see came from her parents. Her parents, though, had a terrible sense of humor, as witnessed in the name they gave her: Phyllis Terra Barnum—P. T. Barnum, for short.

It was a name she didn't mind when she was young because it felt good rolling off the tongue. And it was fun.

But it soon turned into a point of ridicule, especially when the other kids learned its association with clowns, three rings, and very large tents. It became something she sought to live down and wished would just go away.

When she married Jason Turner, though, she decided to keep her family name, a matter of professional intelligence.

As a lecturer on archaeological digs in the American southwest, the name sometimes came in handy, and she took advantage of its associations in her animated deliveries. Because of it, her class lectures were always well-attended and well-received, and her stature amongst her students was strengthened and elevated.

❧   ❧   ❧

Jason was a dreamer—an inventor of gadgets with no previously known purpose and likely no generally accepted use, a writer of haiku in Japanese, and an ardent lover of deep space and the mysteries of the heavens.

16

He completed the Sunday *New York Times* crossword puzzle from memory after viewing it for a mere thirty seconds, working it out totally in his mind—and on the playground he tossed a perfect football spiral with Colleen.

He was notoriously absent-minded.

His work as senior astronomer and director of the NASA—the other NASA—Andromeda Radio Astronomy Center fifty miles southeast of Alamogordo in southern New Mexico took him to interstellar realms well beyond those familiar to most individuals.

His innovative work involving Computer Rendered and Electron-microscopy Enhanced Photographic Imaging (CREEPI for those familiar with it) had won him recognition within an exclusive and close-knit fraternity of radio astronomers and other esoteric scanners of the heavens.

※　　※　　※

Colleen was a dreamer too, and even at her age listened with rapt attention when her father waxed mystically about the birth of stars, the nature of black holes, and the aging of galaxies.

She didn't always have the correct terms, but she spoke intelligently about galactic phenomena (including supernovae, her special interest) to the wonder and delight of her dad's colleagues, who had adopted her as one of their own.

Colleen often accompanied her mother in the field on her special digs, and discovered her first artifact while with her in the Sangre de Cristo Mountains of north-central New Mexico. The primary dig was in a secluded gully, an offshoot of the main river running through an isolated canyon.

Her mother's team had unearthed several ancient relics thought to be left by previous inhabitants of the region, and hopes were high that on closer scrutiny a connection would be established with the Pueblo of old.

Colleen had decided she wanted to explore a little rise beyond the gully, and with her mother's permission had taken trowel and paintbrush to the hillside. When she proudly returned with a flint arrowhead, her mother sent a team back with her to mark her very own dig site.

While nothing else of note emerged from efforts focused on the alternate location, Colleen felt a sense of kinship with her mother's work through that flint artifact, which was returned to the local Pueblo tribe with appropriate identifying nomenclature, date and location of recovery, and the name of the young archaeologist prominently noted.

⌇   ⌇   ⌇

Today, Colleen and her dad had stopped for lunch at this old 18th century hotel in the middle of the stretch of desert between Las Cruces and the White Sands Missile Range. The hotel was a relic of the old west and stood as a charming reminder of that rugged and highly romanticized territory.

The hotel had been refurbished by the owners for the tourist trade, and it wasn't too hard to tell how much of it was authentic and how much commercial retrofit. Colleen, though, was taken with the place. It was quaint, and, she felt, ancient—a place with the feel of time standing still.

This was ancient Pueblo country; it was the land of Coronado and the Seven Cities of Gold; and Colleen felt she'd been here before in another lifetime. She mentioned her feeling to her dad, and he smiled and said he thought he had, too.

At first, Colleen thought he was kidding her, making light of something very real to her. When he held her eyes and said there was a mesa nearby where First Nation Peoples once held their sacred ceremonies and would she like to visit it, she knew he was serious.

It didn't take long to drive to the location, which overlooked a broad river valley.

"How did you know about this place? Did someone at the hotel tell you about it?"

Her dad looked over at her and smiled.

"No, no one there knows about it. I don't know how I knew, exactly. I just sort of pick things up."

They got out of the car and walked a short distance to the edge of the mesa overlooking the valley below. They sat on a low rock near the edge of the canyon and didn't say anything for a while. The silence was palpable, and the sun hovered in the sky, angling toward the west.

⳾   ⳾   ⳾

Jason spoke, breaking the silence: "Coronado was here."

Colleen looked over at her dad. "Why do you say that?"

"Shhh," he said, pointing off into the distance.

Colleen blinked and rubbed her eyes, for there amongst the clusters of trees near the river's edge were riders on horseback, clad in shining breastplates, helmed in steel with lavender plumes fluttering in the breeze, long fire sticks resting across their knees.

She looked over at her father—he was watching the shadowy figures intently.

"Do you see that?" she asked in a whisper.

"Umhmm," he replied, his response coming slowly, eyes fixed on the spot where the figures finally disappeared beyond the bend in the river.

Colleen grabbed her father's hand, and pulling on him said, "We have to go down there, Dad; they're here to see us."

Colleen scrambled down the sloping hillside into the valley below, her dad following close behind. It wasn't very far, and they soon reached the path along the river's edge, fresh hoof prints marking the soft sand.

Jason followed Colleen as she hurried toward the bend in the river they had observed from above. As he came around the bend following her, he was blinded by sunlight reflecting off the river's placid mirrored surface.

Colleen stood transfixed at the water's edge. Jason grabbed her by the shoulders, and drawing her back stepped protectively in front of her.

A large man sat on a huge chestnut horse at the head of a small group of riders. His eyes glared from behind the visor of a steel helmet, and his armor of burnished steel shone in the bright sun, while his hand held the hardwood shaft of a long lance.

His face was set and hard, his beard speckled in light and dark. In spite of his grim visage, his eyes betrayed him as one with a gentle spirit, and Colleen came from behind her father and greeted the man.

She spoke to him in Spanish, saying, "Hello, kind sir!" His eyebrows arched in surprise.

He responded, "Greetings to you, little lady, from the Queen of Spain."

Colleen curtsied, her hazel eyes locked with those of the man. Jason watched, silent and intrigued, his concerns lessening.

The man dismounted from his trusty steed and stood full in front of the two. He lifted the visor of his helmet, exposing eyes like blue-green flashes of light. His lips curled in a wide smile, his face transforming into a plain full of wonderful wrinkles framed in a salt and pepper beard.

Colleen smiled back.

The man knelt, bringing his face level with Colleen. "Who are you, little one?" he asked in Spanish. "And what are you doing in this wilderness without benefit of armor?"

Colleen giggled and responded, "This land isn't so wild or dangerous, and little girls don't wear armor."

"Yet, what of your father?" queried the man, persisting with his questioning. "He is ill-dressed for this land and is without any weapons." The man seemed truly concerned for their safety.

"My father is fine, thank you," answered Colleen. "But, what about you—what are you doing here?"

The man chuckled, and then sighed audibly. "I seek my company of men, who have been gone now for many years in search of the Cities of Gold. Alas, they believed the Cities were close at hand, and left in the dead of night in search of them. Only my trusted few remained with me."

The man's eyes took on a saddened cast at these words, and his proud stance diminished a little.

"We were in the second year of our search, with nary a finding of such Golden Cities as myth would have it," he said. "Many of the men were young and impatient, and their frustration grew. The older men, those who served with me in many campaigns, they, too, grew impatient with the constant unsuccessful searching."

The man paused, and catching Colleen's eyes added, "They left to the last man—with the exception of these. I have been seeking them ever since."

Colleen listened intently. Jason came up behind Colleen and rested his hands on her shoulders. "What is he saying, Honey— what's going on?"

Colleen, without taking her eyes from the man, whispered, "He's searching for his company of men. He says they're somewhere out here looking for the Cities of Gold, and he's been looking for them for a very long time."

The man shifted his weight, still holding his lance.

"The Ancient Peoples who dwell in this region understand the mysteries of the land in ways we do not," said the man quietly. "They have cloaked their Cities of Gold within those mysteries in such ways that neither we nor legions of us will likely discover their locations. Our search goes on too long, and the Queen, our mother, is distressed at the great delay in our return." At this his eyes again took on a saddened cast.

The man sighed deeply. Placing his gloved hand on Colleen's head, he said, "It is best that we be on our way. It is late in the day, and we have but a few hours before nightfall—I do not wish to lose any more time in my search for my company of men. Allegiance to my Queen presses me on."

With that, he turned and mounted his trusty stallion. Wheeling toward the north, he lifted his hand in salute, then spurred his mount forward.

In an instant, he and his band of men were gone around the bend of the river, and the sound of their hoofbeats faded into the silence of the canyon.

Jason and Colleen retraced their steps along the river, and coming to the place where they had earlier descended, climbed the path to the top of the canyon and to their car.

The sun was nearing the western horizon, casting gold and amber hues to the four winds, preparing the earth for the coming of a night of rest.

"What're you thinking, Button?" asked Jason.

Colleen paused for a moment, looking toward the northern horizon. "I hope he finds his men, Dad, so he can finally go home..."

The Whispering Sands
of Kalakoum

Anne watched the grains of sand slip through the pinched waist of the hourglass as the daylight hours edged toward evening. It was still light out, but night was coming on, crickets tuning up their bodies in anticipation of an evening concert.

Anne was fascinated with the tumbling particles of sand as they landed silently atop the growing cone below, while the surface above dimpled and slow-moving grains eased down the sides of glass, then through the upper opening like so much shifting desert sand.

It was truly an "hour" hourglass—she had asked Grandfather to time it one lazy Sunday afternoon, and together they lay on the foot of her bed with the glass and Grandfather's pocket watch with a sweep-second hand.

They talked about a lot of things as they absently watched the falling particles, and Anne remembered it mainly as one of those special times with Grandfather.

When the sand had completely fallen through the opening into the space below, he said it had taken just an hour, give-or-take three seconds.

He was like that—precise. She was six then.

≈   ≈   ≈

Grandfather died a year later following a brief illness, leaving a tremendous hole in her heart. That was four years ago, and Anne still ached from it. She treasured the ancient hourglass, a gift from Grandmother after Grandfather's death, and brought it out whenever she felt a need to think.

The falling sand brought back wonderful memories, and in a soothing way helped her sort things out. This was another of those times. She didn't know exactly what was bothering her, but something just wasn't right.

Anne's mother was on another of her book signing tours, and would be gone for some four weeks. Dad was in Washington, D.C., talking to some people in the government about saving the headwaters of someplace—Anne wasn't quite sure where.

Dad had said the "headwaters" was the place where a river began, and that in itself was intriguing to her.

For now, she was with Grandmother at the ranch until Dad returned on the weekend. Grandmother was just the opposite from Grandfather—she was always talking and had a lot to say about people and what they were like and how things were going for everyone, it seemed.

She wasn't a gossip, at least not in a mean way—she just seemed to know what was going on with people all over, and Anne was always amazed at how much she knew about everyone.

Grandmother shared all this information with a gleam in her eyes and music in her voice, and when she wasn't talking about something she was humming—she did love her music, and did that a lot.

Grandfather was more the strong silent type, and he couldn't hold a candle to Grandmother when it came to talking.

In his own way, though, he would get his word in, even if edgewise. He spoke softly when he spoke, and this always surprised Anne, as he was such a large man.

This didn't mean he wasn't strong, which he was, or didn't have strong ideas or opinions, which he did, but he was more likely to walk softly and hold things in rather than speak his mind.

He had a gleam in his eyes, too, and he whistled absently whenever Grandmother hummed, and they made such a neat pair, Anne thought.

They loved each other very much—that was obvious to Anne. She loved when Grandfather puttered in his garage and tool shed and let her putter with him. She missed that very much now that he was gone.

≥   ≥   ≥

Even though Grandmother had given her permission to putter any time she wanted, it just wouldn't be the same.

Grandmother was in the kitchen, and the aroma of her special chocolate rum cake filled the house. Anne brought out her hourglass and set it on the table at the end of the couch in the family room.

She lay prone on the couch, her chin resting on a well-worn leather arm, her left hand caressing the wood supports of the hourglass, eyes glued to the trickle of sand falling into space.

Soon she was aware only of the falling sand, and the world and its cares were lost in that netherworld of thoughts and dreams unspoken.

Somewhere in the back of her mind she could still hear Grandmother humming, but it became one with the imagined sound of rushing sand as it edged its way down the sides of the upper glass, poised momentarily at the orifice, and leaped into space, tumbling in slow motion through the rarefied air in the expanse of space in the lower glass.

⸜   ⸜   ⸜

Anne opened her eyes and stared up into the dark face of a large man bending over her. She squinted and, holding her hand up, shielded her eyes from the blazing sun. It was very hot, and she felt uncomfortable with her clothes sticking to her.

The man was wearing a long and loose-fitting robe tied at the waist with a heavy gold cord, with a kind of cloth wrapped around his head. It hung down behind him—it too was tied with a golden cord. He was wearing sandals.

He had remarkable brown eyes, and Anne relaxed as he fixed his gaze on her.

"Who are you?" she asked. "And where am I?"

She registered how shaky her voice sounded, and then she anticipated the answer—she was no longer in Kansas.

"I am one named Pellinym," replied the Bedouin, "and you are near the Oasis of Kalakoum, one day's journey by camel to the south of Cairo."

Anne sat up and looked around her. As far as the eye could see there was sand—vast reaches of sand, and very hot.

"Where is Grandmother?" she asked the figure next to her.

"Your grandmother bid you come," came the reply.

Anne's eyes closed slightly, her brow creasing in disbelief tinged with curiosity. "She sent me here?" she queried.

"Yes, little one," said the Bedouin softly. "You were summoned, and your grandmother consented."

"Cairo, you said?" asked Anne, still in disbelief.

The older man smiled and nodded.

"Summoned by whom, and for what?"

The Bedouin laughed out loud. "You are full of questions, little one. But, come—come." He stood up and pointed to a large tent nearby, and putting his finger to his lips motioned for her not to speak but to follow him.

Anne rose and with some difficulty followed him, her feet sinking enough in the sand to make it an effort for her.

He, on the other hand, strode with ease, the result of years of experience on shifting sands, and waited for her at the entrance to the tent. He lifted the tent flap and held it for her as she ducked her head and stepped out of the boiling sun into a darkened interior.

The stark contrast of moving from desert brightness into the shadowed tent was dramatic. For a moment, Anne couldn't see— she stopped and stood still lest she bump into something in the darkness.

"Welcome, Little Florence," said a high-pitched voice.

Anne hesitated, but only a moment, as her eyes now grew accustomed to the low light. "My name is Anne," she countered, looking to the figure across the tent.

"Hmmm," said the voice. "You are known to us here as Florence," came his squeaky reply. "Florence of Arabia..."

Silence.

Anne shifted her weight from one foot to the other, then back again. "No, my name is Anne," she insisted, "from Wyoming."

She heard her voice growing stronger.

The man with the high-pitched voice moved closer to Anne, lifted her chin, and looked into her light hazel eyes. "You have come for some purpose which troubles me," he said.

Anne looked up into his face and saw a wizened old man, his skin sallow and wrinkled, nose crooked and one eye clouded over with a blue film. Shuddering, she stepped back.

Just then the Bedouin, who had been listening at the tent's entrance, stepped forward.

"Mind your manners, Sheik Thelleson," he said, voice just above a whisper but with the force of a thousand winds, his brown eyes glowing fiercely in the semi-light. "The little one has come on my summons and at the release of her grandmother, and you show her little courtesy as her host. How uncivilized and ungracious of you! I brought her here to pay her respects, and this is how you treat her?"

He moved a step closer, and Sheik Nhumb Thelleson retreated to the far side of the tent.

"Who are you to speak to me in this manner?" shrieked the sheik, and he stamped his foot and whined an oath under his breath.

"I am Keeper of Courtesies," said the Bedouin, "an appointment made by your mother."

"Ahh, be you the historian of record as well?" sneered a deep voice from the shadows to the left.

"Bhumble Jhurton, you old camel, you! What brings you out in the light of day?" asked the Bedouin, a twinkle in his voice. "Aren't you afraid being out from under the shadows of your rock?" he added through a hearty laugh.

"This is not a laughing matter, Pellinym," sneered the anemic figure in the shadows.

"Ah, but how can laughter be contained when there is just cause?" returned Pellinym, smiling. "But, enough—we have paid our respects, as is your due." He turned to Anne and, taking her gently by the arm, guided her toward the tent flap and out into the bright sun.

⹊　　⹊　　⹊

Anne ran headlong into a little man rushing into the tent as she was exiting, and the two tumbled to the ground in a jumble of arms and legs.

Anne picked herself up and spit out sand as she brushed herself off. The little man got back on his feet, swore at her and raised his fist, but was stopped by the imposing figure of the Bedouin standing between them.

"So, are you losing your eyesight, Jherqellord?" asked the Bedouin, his voice light and cheerful. "And would you say it is in character for you to strike a young girl, my friend?"

The little man spun around and glared at the Bedouin.

"You mind to your business, camel driver!" sneered the little man, the muscles of his jaw twitching, his eyes dark with rage.

"Come, come, Jherqellord my friend. Where are your manners? You have not yet welcomed our guest. This is Anne Sinclair, sent as an emissary by her grandmother, your contact in the other world."

For the first time, Anne heard a certain quality in the way "Grandmother" was being spoken. Ghuy Jherqellord gasped and moved back a step.

"So you are the one sent from the other side!" whispered the little man. His eyes then grew wide, and he clapped his hand to his forehead, and mumbling under his breath, turned and ducked into the tent.

Anne looked to the tall Bedouin, her eyes puzzled. The man laughed another hearty laugh, and putting his hand on her shoulder the two walked away from the tent a short distance to where the camels were stabled.

Anne walked swiftly, trying to keep pace with the tall Bedouin. She could hear loud shouting coming from the tent they had just left—swear words and angry voices. Anne distinctly felt the cursing and strong language were somehow the result of something she had done or for which she was responsible.

Pellinym looked down into her curious eyes and shook his head. "No, little one, you did nothing to cause the anger in their midst. It springs from something in their pasts, though what I do not know—nor do I hold it of much importance. Surely men of principle, character, and breeding would not treat you so. Your business will be completed despite it."

Anne still looked puzzled. The Bedouin stopped in front of another tent and held the flap aside, nodding for her to enter.

Now what? thought Anne as she once again stepped out of the desert glare into semi-darkness.

"Welcome, Anne," came a voice out of that darkness. As Anne's eyes became accustomed to the dim light, a female figure stepped forward and threw her arms around her.

Anne tried to catch her breath and turned to see who had grabbed her with such affection. "Do I know you?" she asked cautiously.

She was greeted by a striking young woman dressed in flowing lavender silks, a thin gold chain draped around her neck hung with a single elegant pearl.

Anne stepped back, her mind racing. An image in black and white filled her mind's eye, of a young woman standing beside an old Pontiac with her grandfather—they were very young and just married.

The woman's eyes were deep and penetrating, set in a lean face framed in dark hair pulled back loosely, with thinly defined eyebrows and skin of fine alabaster, a slight figure in a summer dress.

"You've guessed rightly, Anne," said Grandmother.

Anne's eyes went wide as she grasped for words. "But, you're so young!" she stammered aloud.

"We are in a place not bound by time," said Grandmother, smiling. "This is Grandfather's home, here in the sands of Kalakoum. He was born here, and it is here he returned to when he left us."

Anne closed her eyes slightly, her brow furrowing. "Grandfather is here?" she asked, excitement just beneath the surface.

"Yes, he has been your guide," the woman said softly, a twinkle in her eyes. Anne turned to face the Bedouin.

As she thought about it, the voice was younger and stronger, but with its gentleness was right, the cut of the jaw familiar.

Then, his eyes settled the matter. Anne ran and leaped into the arms of the huge Bedouin, who hugged her for dear life, and the two laughed and cried.

"Why didn't you say anything?" blurted Anne.

"You know I'm not one for long talks!" he said. Then he chuckled.

"Well, tell me, why am I here?" asked Anne of her grandparents.

"You've been summoned to help with a slight problem," said Grandmother softly.

She smiled, with that light in her eyes that always comforted Anne when things got a bit too weird around home.

"But, who summoned me, and for what?" pressed Anne.

"Your question of 'why' is more to the point than 'who' or 'what,'" said Grandfather.

"Then, why?" asked Anne again as she looked into Grandfather's eyes.

"You have the hourglass I gave you when Grandfather left us," said Grandmother. Anne nodded, her eyes holding those of the young woman.

"You did something rare amongst people—you put yourself into the mind of a grain of sand," the woman said. "You allowed yourself to glide down the hourglass's side, and at the primordial edge flung yourself into space. In that moment light and dark became one."

Anne closed her eyes ever so slightly, her mind taking in the words of her beautiful grandmother.

Grandfather added, "The people of the desert know many things, but those two men know not the secret of a grain of sand as you do."

Grandfather beamed, his pearly teeth gleaming in the subdued light within the tent.

"What secret are you talking about?" queried Anne, puzzled.

Grandfather put his hand on Anne's shoulder. "It is the simple truth that everything in the universe is connected to every other thing. By the way, given how you have been treated since your arrival it is clear these men do not comprehend this simple truth. If they did, they would treat you very differently," he concluded.

"What am I supposed to do with that?" Anne asked.

"Your presence is all that is needed, little one," whispered the huge Bedouin. "That power already has offset the dark influences of discourtesy and uncivilized tongues. You have done well, indeed."

Anne took Grandmother's and Grandfather's hands in hers. As they exited the tent into the brightness outside, Anne closed her eyes slightly. Her gaze fixed on a stream of sand falling through space in slow motion.

Light was darkness, and shadows and brightness were one and the same. She heard Grandmother's humming mixed with the background rushing of sand sliding down glass, and then that leap into space—now, tumbling, floating down softly, coming to rest on a growing cone of sand...

Sugar and Spice, Everything Nice

Mandy hurried along passageway T-7 in the third tier of space station Orion. Dante trotted alongside her with ease, his collar clinking in the early morning silence. It was always quiet throughout the space station at 5:00 A.M., and the guards never patrolled this sector before 7 o'clock.

Dante projected a thought warning to Mandy as they approached the corner near the health center, and she thought back a *Thanks* to him as she felt the walls with her mind and turned left down passageway T-6.

Dante knew that at the end of this passage was the station's garden complex, where Mandy often went when she wanted to be alone. This was not a garden as such, but a place of special wonders—of grassy hillsides and sunny fields, craggy purple mountains with rushing whitewater rivers, and sometimes the shifting sandcliffs of the fifth moon of Daarvan, the dark and melancholy crylenium mines of Percephane, or the crystalline beaches of Lake Meridium high in the mountains of the planet Khorsov.

Dante always went with her during her mind-walks and loved their time together. Being a dog, he wasn't very good himself at this mind-walk thing, so he valued the opportunity of going with her to learn.

❧   ❧   ❧

Today, Mandy was meeting Perch, her best friend, next to Dante, of everyone on the space station. Perch was sixteen, just two years older then herself and the only person who could hear her thought projections. He was also the only one who could hear Dante when he mind-spoke. They were inseparable, these three dearest friends. Today Perch said they had to meet in the garden because the space station was under general lockdown.

Mandy felt the button panel with her mind, keyed in the code and opened the outer door to the airlock, then the inner door, and the two slipped into quad-4 of the garden complex.

The birds were beginning to chirp in that time just before sunrise, and there was a slight breeze blowing from the eastern mountains. Perch had described that region once as "the land of mystery, east of the soul"; the description stuck for Mandy.

It was a beautiful morning, but Mandy was anxious to see Perch and so hurried herself along. She sensed the rough surface of the trail with her mind, as she felt the dirt and pebbles under her feet. She walked smoothly along the path, sensing the changes and turns in her mind's eye. Dante kept pace with her as she moved effortlessly along the pathway.

"Hi hi," called a voice from behind. Perch had entered quad-4 just after the duo and caught up with them near the old cypress tree.

Mandy reached out her hands, and Perch took them and squeezed hard. Dante said *Hi,* too, and jumped up to lick Perch's face. Mandy knew something was troubling Perch, so she projected, *What's on your mind?*

Perch smiled and said, "We shouldn't talk here. We need to get farther up the hillside."

Soon they came to an overlook just above the river and, finding a sheltered place away from the path, sat down.

So, what's up? thought Mandy.

Perch asked excitedly, "Mandy, have you heard the news?"

Mandy thought back, *No, what news?*

Perch explained that the security police were gathering up all personal computers and impounding them—even the obsolete wristwatch PCs.

"It's a control thing," said Perch. "A group of kids have been getting into the main system, and there have been problems. Trohl Nhevil, director of Orion Security, authorized the sweep of Orion early this morning. Jurquil Bhodi, Nhevil's assistant, was the one primarily handling today's raid. By now they've already gathered up most of the computers on the space station."

Perch paused, then said, "When I learned of the sweep, I tried to hide my wallet PC in the shaft of the crylenium mines, but they had followed me and easily confiscated it."

Mandy thought, *Mine was in my room. If they started this morning, they probably already have it by now.*

"Too bad," said Perch. Dante just snuffled and harrumphed.

Mandy projected to Perch, *It doesn't matter, I rarely used it anyway.*

Puzzled, Perch asked, "How do you do anything without it?"

Mandy smiled and thought, *I haven't needed it for a long time.*

Nope! thought Dante. *Hasn't.*

Perch was really puzzled now, so Mandy thought, *I use my thoughts for almost everything.*

She does, thought Dante.

Yep! No one can access what I think, thought Mandy. *Now come on, I want to show you something.* She got up and rushed down the path toward the garden entrance. Perch raced after her, with Dante loping alongside.

They came racing out the airlock doors of the garden complex and narrowly missed crashing into the garden director, who was just arriving, along with a squad of guards patrolling D-6.

Perch's eyes widened when he saw that the leader of the patrol was Jurquil Bhodi.

Bhodi grabbed Mandy's arm and yelled for the guards to hold the two. He directed Mandy to keep her dog under control, or his mind would be erased.

Mandy caught Dante's inner ear with one word: *Mind.*

Dante sat back on his haunches beside Mandy.

Perch struggled as the guards held his arms to his sides.

"What were you doing in D-6/0707?" Bhodi hissed.

Perch explained, "We were just watching the sunrise on Darvaan, that's all."

"How did you get in?" hissed Bhodi.

Tell him some idiot left the door unlocked, thought Dante.

"Quiet," whispered Perch.

Mandy quickly thrust out her open hand, which held a small plastic card.

"Aha—why do you still have this key?" asked Bhodi. "Why wasn't it turned in when the recall was issued?"

Tell the idiot she liked the pretty colors! thought Dante.

Perch stepped on Dante's tail and muttered, "I said quiet!"

Perch explained that Mandy was blind and couldn't speak, adding she didn't know the keys had been recalled because she just last night returned to Orion from a visit with her parents.

Dante licked his tail where Perch had stepped on it and gave him a dirty look.

Bhodi looked through narrowed eyelids at Perch, his eyes

gleaming with a hardness that sent chills down Perch's spine. Perch tried not to flinch, or blink; it was with effort that he held Bhodi's gaze.

Bhodi grabbed the key from Mandy's hand.

"Curfew isn't over until 7:00 A.M. What are you doing out without a permit?" Bhodi's voice dropped, taking on a more ominous tone.

Perch began to perspire. He stammered, but then was silent.

The guard standing behind Perch interrupted Bhodi, indicating that according to the master computer a visit to D-6/0707 in the name of "Grosvenor, P." had been cleared for this morning.

Bhodi looked at the two and their dog with anger in his eyes. "On your way, and stay out of trouble!" he snarled.

※ ※ ※

As they rushed along the hallway, Perch asked Mandy if she had requested a permit.

No, thought back Mandy, *I didn't. Did you?*

"No," said Perch. "I don't get it. Who did?" A large hand reached out to grab and yank on his ponytail, jerking him off-balance. Perch tumbled onto the floor, arms and legs flying.

He looked up to see Trohl Nhevil's angry face glaring down at him.

"What can you tell me about the communications graffiti problem, Mister Grosvenor?" Nhevil emphasized the *Mister Grosvenor.*

Perch tried to get up, but Nhevil put his foot on Perch's chest and pinned him to the floor. Perch said, "I don't know what you're talking about!" but Nhevil persisted, accusing him of entering coded messages into the space station's intercom.

Perch knew that over the past few months several unauthorized messages had been broadcast over the communications monitors.

Some of these transmissions were curious, but most were disconnected from the usual fare of intercom messages.

Perch vigorously denied anything to do with the messages. He had, however, the reputation of being a self-taught computer genius; he was extremely bright, and with a creative bent had broken and deciphered the super codes of the Orion's operating computers.

He'd gotten into not just a little trouble over that. Even Orion's technical consultants on occasion had asked Perch's assistance with some perplexing software problems. Because of this, and because Nhevil didn't like Perch's attitude, he believed that Perch was the culprit behind the annoying and illegal intercom messages.

Nhevil growled, "I have you under surveillance, so be very careful!" With that he turned and angrily strode down the hall toward central security.

Mandy asked about these intercom messages that she'd missed, and Perch said he could only remember a few. The first was short and sweet: "Tyranny is a four-letter word..."

But tyranny isn't a four-letter word! thought Dante.

"Someone, and nobody knows who, obviously is upset with our dear director Nhevil. Another went something like, 'Dream, and the unimagined becomes possible...' The one I liked best went, '*Why?* is the most irritating weapon of the oppressed, *I am* the most potent...' And then last week Nhevil went ballistic after, 'The heart is the pump of the body—it is also the pump of Courage, Inquiry, and Freedom...'"

❧   ❧   ❧

Mandy thought, *Who could be doing this?*

Perch shrugged. He hadn't the vaguest idea.

"Everyone across Orion is talking about these messages, and

because Nhevil as director of Orion Security can't stop them, most people have been laughing at him and the whole comic situation—well, not to his face, but it is pretty funny. Of course this angered Nhevil all the more, and he vowed he would take all means necessary to apprehend the computer terrorist. It is curious and intriguing, because breaching computer security is no mean feat! Whoever's doing this is some super crafty spirit who knows a little something about electronic wizardry. And he, or she, is waxing philosophical, and has a devilish sense of humor."

Mandy smiled in agreement. *It is pretty funny!* she thought. *Was the broadcast with "freedom" the most recent one?*

Perch replied, "This hacker got through the secret codes and entered another phantom message at communications central last night, but it was blocked before going out over the system."

Do you know what the message was? thought Mandy.

"It said 'Life is like...'" Perch started.

...a box of chocolates... finished Dante.

*With apologies to Forrest Gump

Midnight Sun Rising

Snowy Owl banked to his left and caught the updraft coming off the butte overlooking the river. He could feel the weather changing—the long endless winter night was drawing to a close, and the land was beginning to emerge from its peaceful slumber.

Below him, Arctic Wolf was padding along a well-beaten path alongside the river. Caribou herds had cut this path through the snows early last fall, using it to cross the low-lying tundra plains.

Wolf was exhausted because of the sparse foraging late into the extended Arctic night. This was the life of a lone predator in the frozen wilds.

Snowy Owl and Wolf were longtime friends, though Snowy Owl knew to keep a respectful distance when it came to Wolf. Wolf didn't mind Snowy Owl's caution—he imagined he would do the same were their circumstances reversed.

He often wondered what it would be like to glide silently on the night air, seeing one's prey from on high, then swooping down with nary a sound until your sharp talons grasped your quarry and you eased up into the chill night air once again.

Wolf's life was difficult by comparison. The long night of the hunt took its toll because the herds were small and the snows deep. The deep snows slowed his pursuit, and it was cold and dirty work.

Wolf didn't mind, for his line had long hunted the Arctic wastes, and while winter was often harsh, it was a good life. This was home.

❧   ❧   ❧

Snowy Owl swooped down and silently floated up behind Wolf, whose vigilant ears missed his approach. Wolf padded on effortlessly. With that sixth sense, he turned and caught movement out of the corner of his eye.

There was Snowy Owl. The two moved together across the tundra in the growing light.

Snowy Owl liked Wolf. Theirs was a unique relationship that began when Wolf's mother saved Snowy Owl from certain death at the jaws of a band of renegade wolves. Snowy Owl's mother had been killed by the wolf leader, and just as he moved in on his little prey, Wolf's mother stepped in and would not let any pass.

This was unheard of. Snowy Owl escaped a cold fate and felt nothing but gratitude to Wolf's mother.

Often Arctic Wolf would be seen racing across the tundra in pursuit of an animal, while above Snowy Owl flew circles in some form of sympathetic union with Wolf until he caught his prey.

After Wolf finished his meal, he left aside a portion for Snowy Owl. Snowy Owl, though, did not accept any of the gifts left for him by Wolf—he couldn't go that far.

He did, however, understand Wolf, and appreciated the gesture for what it was. Wolf grasped that Snowy Owl couldn't accept the gift of food left from the hunt, and didn't take it personally, but continued to leave portions for his close yet distant friend.

❧   ❧   ❧

Willow Ptarmigan—Will to those who knew him—loved the long Arctic winters. He delighted in that sense of endless time, the quality of perfect stillness of the Arctic during these periods of sundown.

The hues of the Arctic night were magical—lavenders, purples, and blues bordering on black, the shades of the underside of midnight.

And the wonder of night flight required that sixth sense that birds of the Arctic owned, permitting the hunt during the extended winter's night.

Will was a distant cousin of Snowy Owl. He, too, liked Arctic Wolf, and like Snowy Owl, caution dictated he maintain a safe distance.

Will wouldn't join in the hunt with Wolf, although he was fascinated and watched from a distance. Even to watch from above, as did Snowy Owl, felt too close for him, but he didn't judge Snowy Owl for his involvement.

He marveled at Wolf's prowess, and with not a little bit of fear.

Wolf left portions of his kills for Will, too, and Will didn't miss the fact. Like Snowy Owl, Will couldn't bring himself to accept these gifts. Never in all his family's history did a Wolf have a coexistent relationship with a Ptarmigan; it just never happened.

Will didn't try to make anything more of it than that it happened, and that Wolf was just another creature in the harsh Arctic wilds making a go of things, surviving.

Survival was very dear to all creatures in the north. Defy nature, and the price was eternal sleep, a state of permanent midnight sun.

Nome Teleson cinched the wide belt of his parka tighter to block out the wind, also pulling the drawstring of his hood close around his face.

The wind had picked up, causing a drop in temperature. It was beginning to rain; any colder and the drops would turn to snow. Then they would have to delay their departure.

He climbed into the back seat of the bush plane, joining his party, and shortly the thundering engine propelled the aircraft down the runway and into the chill air. Soon the buildings and lights of Fairbanks were behind them, and the pilot reached for altitude.

Teleson was a renowned Alaskan wilderness guide, who came by his skill and reputation through grit, determination, and a native intelligence in aces.

However, life in the north was hard for Teleson, and he did not fare well. Short-suited in his inner self, he also had a dislike for people. This was generally not a good thing for a wilderness guide.

Early on he learned that to survive, one had to climb over others or bring them down. He learned this lesson well and felt no qualms in advancing his cause in life at the expense of all others.

He was known for his sharp tongue, and exhibited no mercy when it came to pouring his venom out at the expense of others. This he did easily, and with little discrimination—his vitriol was equal opportunity.

In the back seat next to Teleson sat his longtime partner, Bimbeau Juhrtone, a reclusive French-Canadian hunting guide, expert in the ways of Arctic creatures and the means needed to bring them down.

He was sickly, given to a tubercular condition that had plagued him off and on, and which wracked his frail body when he coughed.

His senses, though, were ever sharp, keen in discerning the slightest shifts in the weather, and observing of minute changes in the ways of creatures of the northern wilds—the better to know their intimate wanderings, and their ultimate weaknesses.

Teleson and Juhrtone trafficked in the trade of those who hunt not for utility, as for food or clothing, but for sport—for those obscene masculine trophies that graced the dens of the wealthy.

Ghuy Jailor sat in the seat next to the pilot. This was his first trip to the northern wilderness of Alaska. He came to "bag a big one," as they said in the inner smoking rooms of his exclusive business club back in Chicago.

He looked down and saw a meandering river cutting through rough terrain, with rocky crags reaching up past the plane's wings on both sides.

"Damn, they're close!" he shouted, but his words were lost in the explosion of sound inside the plane's cabin.

He had selected the seat next to the pilot, a place of importance in his mind, and now was trying not to look afraid.

He was brought roughly back to the present when the plane caught a sudden downdraft and his stomach rammed up into his throat. He gasped, and the knuckles of both hands holding the seat belt turned even whiter.

Winds buffeted the plane, tossing it about wildly, and the bolts of the old workhorse creaked and groaned, giving the occupants good cause for worry.

Their bush pilot seemed oblivious of their imminent deaths. Teleson and Juhrtone clutched their armrests with such force the plane seemed to groan all the more.

They were certain they were going to crash into the side of a glacier.

Suddenly the plane nosed down, and clouds whipped past, beads of rain driven by the force of the descent toward the tail of the plane.

"We're going to die!" screamed Juhrtone against the roar of wind and engine.

"Arrrrgh!" came a cry from deep within Teleson, as he felt his trousers grow warm and a trickle run down his right leg.

Jailor's eyes grew large, and his mouth opened wide, but no sound came forth.

≫   ≫   ≫

The pilot was calm, eyeing the mountainous terrain as earth and thunder came rushing up to engulf them.

His hand was rock steady as he guided the bush plane down into the valley, while his eyes sought a stretch of gravel to serve as a landing strip.

With the wind howling and his passengers screaming, one silently, the pilot pulled out of his dive, leveling off just at the last moment. The plane's huge tires slammed down onto the gravel sandbar.

The plane bumped and jounced, water and debris splashing on the undersides of the wings, and after an interminable stretch came to a halt. Even with the howling of the winds and slashing of the rains outside, it seemed deathly quiet inside the plane's cabin.

They were safely down.

The bush pilot helped a shaken Ghuy Jailor from the plane as two equally shaken wilderness guides climbed out onto the gravel airstrip.

The pilot smiled as he unloaded the backpacks, food, equipment, one large gun case, and a deflated river raft.

The rain continued in slashing torrents, and a fierce wind blew out of the north. The pilot shouted to Jailor above the roar of the gusts that he would pick them up at the mouth of the river on the Beaufort Sea in three weeks and wished them well.

Lifting off from the makeshift airstrip, he circled twice and dipped his wings, chuckling as he flew off to the west toward Fairbanks.

Juhrtone and Teleson worked quickly to erect their tents in order to get out of the rain.

Once that was completed, Teleson worked steadily to set up the cook tent, which would serve also as the dining tent and protection against the hordes of mosquitoes that lurked just beyond sight, waiting to pounce when the rain stopped.

"There's a wolf beyond the ridge!" shouted Ghuy Jailor as he stumbled into camp. Juhrtone and Teleson dropped what they were doing and, grabbing their powerful weapons, raced for the ridge to the south of camp.

Both were in better condition than Jailor, but both struggled on their approach to the crest of the hill.

They dropped to their knees and crawled slowly to a vantage point giving a sweeping view of the side of the hill opposite the riverbend.

There in the open near the river's edge was a dark figure that the two men quickly identified as a large Arctic wolf.

Curiously, the wolf was followed in the air by two birds, looking like mere dots from this distance. Teleson guessed they were peregrine falcons.

Slowly, Juhrtone and Teleson moved down the hillside, gliding silently from one rock to another, from behind one mound to another.

Here their skills became evident. As they approached within a hundred yards of the wolf, Teleson took up a position behind a low stone outcropping, his powerful rifle propped up on a rock.

He adjusted the powerful scope, accounting for the distance to his quarry, and viewed through the eyepiece.

The early morning shadows gave way to a highlighted image, a fine crosshair at the center of the scope's viewing area now resting on a spot just behind the shoulder of the grey wolf. Teleson sucked in his breath, breathed out just a little, and held it.

He gently squeezed the trigger, but before he could complete the action the vision in the scope was blurred by a flurry of wings, a loud screeching piercing his ears. Sudden shocking pain shook his left hand, which cradled the rifle.

Teleson screamed and jumped back, dropping his powerful weapon.

Juhrtone whined aloud, being attacked by a frenzied Willow Ptarmigan, and swung his rifle around, firing several wild shots that narrowly missed Teleson.

Teleson yelled, "Juhrtone, stop shooting!" and screamed again as Snowy Owl's talons narrowly missed his eyes.

With an unnerving squawk, Will Ptarmigan beat his wings about the head of a babbling Juhrtone, who, flailing his arms about to ward off the flying attack, soiled himself.

Suddenly, Arctic Wolf leaped over the low rock formation and into the fray, snarling with teeth bared.

Juhrtone threw down his weapon and fled down the hillside toward the river, arms waving madly about.

Teleson screamed a curdling wail and, beating with his arms while warding off the grey wolf, also scrambled back to the river.

Ghuy Jailor, who had been watching the scene unfold, picked himself up and fled in the other direction.

∗   ∗   ∗

Wolf loped down the hillside, howling, snarling, and snapping his jaws, now more for effect, adding to the fright of his would-be assailants in their flight to safety.

Snowy Owl dropped down onto a low mound at the foot of the hill and chuckled. Will feathered his wings and came to rest beside his companion.

Wolf padded silently back and sat a safe distance from Snowy Owl and Will.

"Thank you," he said, his eyes alternately holding those of his two friends.

"It was nothing," Will replied.

"Yes," added Snowy Owl.

Shadows in the Galaxies

Alli moved through the room with ease, and other than a furtive glance from someone at the far table, no one took notice of her. It was quiet in the way that libraries are quiet, with a hint of echoes bouncing off the high vaulted ceilings. You could almost hear the books breathing.

The quiet was offset by rushing wind and the pelting of hard-driven rains on the outside of tall windows above the shelves in the reference room.

The lights dimmed ever so slightly as lightning flashed across the darkened skies outside. The room was lit by the low lights on the tables, giving the room a closed-in cozy feeling. It was a perfect day to be indoors, and Alli was glad to be here.

The reference room was a special place for Alli. It was a haven that drew her whenever she was feeling restless. And today was no different—today she was looking for information on powerful women figures in history.

She moved her wheelchair close to the computer console and tapped in her library card number, followed by her password. Then she tapped in the eight-digit code for the series on Historic Women Power Figures and waited as the processor handled her request.

The silver-white glow of the monitor screen blinked as the processor completed a dozen steps in a matter of milliseconds.

She knew where the musty tomes of this series were kept on the fourth floor, but with the installation of computer terminals, she could now peruse at the console rather than traversing those narrow aisleways on the upper floors of the library.

⁎　⁎　⁎

Today Alli wanted only to look through the table of contents volume, and then she would visit the fourth floor and actually turn the pages of the books—there was something satisfying about touching and turning actual pages rather than swiping the screen.

Her fingers flew over the keyboard, tapping out the necessary instructions. She found a likely section in the third chapter of Volume VI under the title "Royal Women and Decision-Making."

With this information Alli moved over to the elevator. She pulled the old metal door open and swung the sliding grate aside, then rolled herself into the small cubicle.

The grate slid shut behind her. She maneuvered her chair around in the tight space, pushed the button for the fourth floor, and waited. There was a momentary pause as the old motor above whirred into action, and the elevator lurched upward amid the old building's creaks and groans.

Alli leaned back, watching the floor numbers alternately lighting up and turning off as the elevator approached and passed each floor. The elevator jerked slightly as it drew near the fourth floor, and the floor number blinked on and off several times before going off altogether. Alli registered this somewhere in the back of her mind but paid no heed.

Alli pulled on the sliding grate, but it stuck. She pulled harder, and it jerked free and banged loudly against the elevator frame. She pushed the door open and started out of the elevator.

When the elevator stopped it came to rest slightly above its normal position, leaving a drop from the elevator to the floor outside. As Alli rolled out of the elevator, the front wheels of her wheelchair dropped down some eight inches, pitching her forward.

Alli landed hard on her knees and upper torso, her arms coming up to protect herself. Her head hit the floor hard, and pain blurred her vision. Then everything went black.

⚞ ⚞ ⚞

Alli could make out low murmuring, and heard her name being spoken. When she opened her eyes everything was still black, and her head throbbed. She tried to sit up and found herself in a dark place with a musty smell. The floor was damp and cold. She looked around for her wheelchair, then for the elevator door.

It was dark, and though her eyes were still getting use to the low light, she could see that her wheelchair wasn't anywhere in sight. The elevator was gone, and she seemed to be in some dank cave.

She called out to whomever was talking to come and help her, and the murmuring immediately stopped. Then two heads popped from around the corner.

Alli looked long and hard at the two heads—one was a large rabbit with long floppy ears and remarkable green eyes. The other head was of an equally large cat, with banded stripes of orange and light grey across its shoulders. It, too, had remarkable eyes. Both grinned big smiles at Alli as they came around the corner and sat down beside her.

"Hi," said the cat. "My name is Chelsie, and as you can see I am a cat."

"Hello," said the rabbit, "you can call me Latté." He smiled broadly.

Alli was at a loss for words, and the two creatures chuckled at her puzzlement. She was upset that they were laughing at her and hadn't offered to help.

"Would you help me up?" she asked. "And would you help find my wheelchair?"

The two creatures continued to laugh, made a joke, and laughed some more.

Then the rabbit said, "You know, you can come with us the way you are."

Alli looked up at him and said, "No, not without my wheels."

The cat smiled and said, "Oh, yes you can!" He turned to leave.

The rabbit chimed in, "Of course you can; of course, you did."

Alli looked at them both with a frown and said, "Stop teasing me!"

The rabbit's eyes glowed, and he spoke in a quiet yet deliberate tone: "Of course you have; of course, you were."

He smiled broadly, grasped Alli's arm and nodded to the cat, who came around to the other side and grasped Alli's other arm. Together they struggled and eventually lifted her to her feet.

She wobbled, and grabbed tightly to their arms—actually, to their forepaws. Then the two let Alli's arms go and stepped back.

Alli's eyes grew large, and she gasped and put her arms out to catch her fall, but she didn't fall. She could feel the muscles of her feet and legs and upper body tighten just so, responding to latent memory traces. While a bit wobbly, she remained standing.

She looked into the rabbit's eyes, then the cat's, and opened her mouth to speak.

"Here you are you, nothing more, nothing less," said the rabbit with a gleam in his eyes. The cat grinned widely and nodded. Alli took several steps, still a bit wobbly, but steps nevertheless. She smiled before grabbing and hugging the two furry creatures, whose eyes bugged out a bit from being squeezed.

$$\approx \qquad \approx \qquad \approx$$

Suddenly, there came a loud commotion from outside the cave, with a lot of yelling.

They rushed to the cave entrance, though it took Alli a bit longer to get there than the other two.

Outside, in a clearing near the cave entrance, stood a crocodile with fierce yellow eyes opposite an angry-looking hyena, both yelling at the top of their lungs. Alli couldn't understand what they were saying, but they seemed quite angry.

The rabbit whispered to Alli that this was Ti-Ehn, the crocodile from the lower Nile. His nasty compatriot, the one with the terrible taste in clothes, was Jaibee the hyena.

"Why are they so angry?" asked Alli.

"Oh, they're just being critical. They criticize all the time, everything and everyone," said Latté.

"And they don't seem to be able to help it, poor things!" chimed in Chelsie.

"What do they criticize?" asked Alli.

"As we said, everyone and everything."

At the sound of their voices Ti-Ehn stopped his screaming. He pointed a gnarled finger at the three in the mouth of the cave and snarled, "You have done wrong! You have committed a grave error! The Queen cannot save you!"

Alli pulled back into the shadows of the cave and whispered, "What does he mean?"

"Oh, he makes that all up—don't you worry," replied Chelsie. "He's as crazy as that fool with the silly grin, so don't worry your pretty little head!"

"And he's just a meanie," added Latté. "The Queen will take care of him." He then called out to Ti-Ehn and Jaibee, "Be off with you—on the Queen's orders!"

Ti-Ehn snarled and snapped his jaws in Latté's direction.

Jaibee, too, snarled and snuffled, but more at the air than anything else; he seemed to be lost in another world.

Latté recoiled and mumbled under his breath.

"Be off, I say! The Queen will not be happy," mocked the rabbit.

"No, no! She will not!" Chelsie grinned and nodded agreement.

Suddenly, there was another commotion in their midst, and Jaibee yelled to Ti-Ehn, "The Queen is coming!"

Ti-Ehn froze, and his yellow eyes narrowed. He looked over his shoulder in the direction of the path to the river. Soldiers in armor were running along the pathway, and there was much yelling and calling out of orders, and men on horseback rode furiously through the rushing madness.

There was chaos and confusion, and dust flew everywhere. The soldiers formed a circle around the cornered crocodile and his chuckling cohort. Then all fell silent.

Ti-Ehn slapped Jaibee across the snout. Jaibee stopped laughing and snarled and snuffled. Ti-Ehn looked the Captain of the Guard in the eye, spat, and laughed out loud.

"Off with their heads!" came a thundering cry from the direction of the river. "Off with their heads!"

Out of the clouds of dust that still swirled around the gathered group strode a formidable figure dressed in regal finery, the crest of a red heart emblazoned across her chest.

Her hair was flowing, the color of gold, and on her head rested the bejeweled crown of the Queen.

"Off with their heads," she bellowed again, eyeing the two inside the ring of soldiers. A shudder ran down Jaibee's spine, a trickle down his leg.

Ti-Ehn roared and snapped in the direction of the Queen, but this was an empty gesture, and he seemed to know it. The Queen held Ti-Ehn's gaze and froze him in place. Ti-Ehn blinked and caught his breath.

Then, without batting an eyelid, the Queen pointed in the direction of the river, and the Captain of the Guard moved to Ti-Ehn's side. Grasping his arm, he shoved him in the direction of the silently flowing waters.

Alli watched in rapt attention. Slowly, the crocodile moved along the pathway, followed by a whimpering Jaibee. The Captain of the Guard followed next, a lance with a gleaming razor-sharp tip prodding the two meanies.

"Off with their heads!" bellowed the Queen as she followed this procession. Then she chuckled, almost to herself.

"What will they do with them?" asked Alli. "Will they hurt them?"

"Oh, no," said Latté. "The Queen is really not a meanie herself."

"She says that all the time, but only because it sounds frightening," said Chelsie. "She doesn't really mean it."

"What will happen to them?" asked Alli.

"Oh, dear," said Latté excitedly. "It's past the time! It's past the time!"

"The time for what?" asked Alli. "What's wrong?"

Chelsie grinned. "Latté was supposed to be at a party yesterday, and now he can't get there until tomorrow."

"Did my coming make him late?" asked Alli.

"Oh, no," said Chelsie. "He's never on time to anything, anyway. Besides, here in the Queen's realm there is never a time that is right, and one is never on time for anything. But then, one is never late for anything, either."

The rabbit smiled. "No, you didn't make me late."

Suddenly, the world around them began to shimmer, and the ground moved. Everything swirled round and around, and the light around them dimmed. Then everything went black.

Silence.

Alli lifted her head. It hurt. She opened her eyes and found herself looking up into the face of a woman with incredible deep blue eyes.

"Are you all right?" she asked Alli. "I heard you take a tumble and found you here in front of the elevator. You have a nasty bump on your head. The paramedics are on their way."

Alli pulled herself to a sitting position, and her arm brushed the frame of her wheelchair. She tried to stand, but her legs wouldn't move. As she struggled, the woman put a hand on Alli's shoulder and said, "You should wait until the paramedics come before trying to get up."

Alli nodded and leaned back against her wheelchair.

The woman handed Alli a handkerchief she'd moistened from the water fountain, and suggested she hold it against the bump on her head. Then the woman left.

Alli looked down at the handkerchief. It had an embroidered emblem in one corner, a red heart...

Snakes and Snails, and Puppy Dog Tails

Allyson was a precocious ten-year-old, innocent as a newborn but a soul older than the granite in the hillside behind her grandfather's house. Her eyes were deep pools that lit up at the thought of journeys to ancient or exotic lands, visitations by angels, or rummaging through the old trunks and wardrobes in her grandparents' attic.

Today it was raining hard, and Allyson's grandfather had to go into town, so he couldn't explore with her. Her grandmother was puttering in the kitchen, and heavenly smells came wafting up the stairs, mixed with the strains of some Verdi opera.

This was like a second home to Allyson. Outside it was much too wet and cold, and the chill would cut right through you before you took half a dozen steps into the backyard. So today she was inside, anticipating visiting another world, being transported to places beyond the stars, and she was happy.

Allyson always had permission to go up to the attic, and she never refused her calling when she visited with Gram and Grampa. The attic was her special place, and they knew that.

The third stair creaked as she climbed the last flight up to the dusty brown door. The doorknob was ancient crystal, a gift, she said, of the Sultan of Bündalaar, from the planet Sämar in the Trinian Galaxy. Usually, it sparkled as sunlight shown through the octagon-shaped window above the staircase, touching it and its brass collar, but today the storm outside made the stairway dark enough that she had to turn on the hall light.

She turned the knob and pushed the door gently. It swung open as smooth as silk, until it banged lightly against the old dresser. The floorboards creaked as she padded in her slippers—creak, swish, creak, swish. The sound of the rain against the roof filled the musty room with a familiar vibration.

It was dark in spite of the floor lamp that stood to the side of the wardrobe, but it was warm and cozy, with sweet smells and heavenly music in the air—everything was familiar, so Allyson felt safe.

She sat down for a moment in Grampa's old rocking chair that her great-grandmother had brought from the old country. It was a special chair, and it felt good to be cradled in its smooth arms. It gave an impression to Allyson of being from some faraway place. She uncurled from the chair and ran her hand over the surface of the dresser, feeling its fine hand-varnished surface. The wood felt warm to the touch. Yes, this was home—her home beyond never.

Allyson stood in front of the freestanding full-length mirror and smiled at herself reflected through a filmy layer of dust. Allyson waited, but just for a moment, and then *she* appeared in the reflection beside her. Allyson turned and looked into the dark eyes of the woman, then reached up and hugged her hard.

She was dressed in long flowing fabrics, soft to the touch, silky, and feeling of the warmth of the sun. "Are you ready?" the woman asked.

"Oh, yes," said Allyson. Taking Allyson by the hand they walked to the dusty trunk in the corner. Allyson lifted the lid, and they both stepped in and scrunched down.

Allyson pulled the trunk lid closed, and they were dashed into darkness blacker than midnight. She always loved the soft swishing sounds she heard on these journeys, and this time was no different. In time the noise softened, gradually died down, and then all was silent. The woman whispered softly into Allyson's ear, and Allyson nodded, said, "Yes," and pushed the lid up, opening it to bright sunlight.

Allyson found herself at the edge of a magical forest where the trees were dark and forbidding, and the bright sunlight did nothing to lessen their pall. She could feel a tension in the air, and she didn't like that. All of a sudden, out of the trees came racing a large furry rabbit wearing a green vest, who careened between the bushes and around rocks and over fallen trees.

The rabbit was chased by two powerful-looking dogs of the mongrel type. The larger dog's teeth were bared and flashing in the sunlight. Its eyes flared red as deep as field poppies. It howled an eerie moan, bone-chilling as something heard in a dank old graveyard, and its muscles rippled under its short tan fur.

The second dog was smaller but more powerfully built. He was limping because of a deformed right paw, but in spite of this kept pace with the first dog.

The rabbit came flying around the last tree at the edge of the forest and ran smack into Allyson. It flopped on its back from the impact but hurriedly picked itself up, leaping into Allyson's protective arms.

The two dogs slid to a halt before Allyson and, snarling, lunged at the ball of fur protected in her arms.

Allyson stood as tall as she could and turned to shield the rabbit with her body.

The dogs snarled and leaped and snapped, but Allyson was steadfast and wouldn't let them near the bunny.

Then a smallish slightly built man rode up on a massive horse, pulling up alongside Allyson and the two frenzied dogs. He barked a command, and the two dogs stopped and fell to beside the rider.

Allyson looked up into the broad face of the man, into his large blue-grey eyes, but before she could say a word he said he was sorry if his dogs had frightened her. He dismounted and introduced himself as the king of the forest. These were his guards, Toomer and Jason, who were chasing this enemy of the realm.

Allyson protested, "But this is a mere bunny!"

The king smiled a most benevolent smile and said, "Yes, he certainly has that appearance."

The king continued, "This is Rudolfo, the notorious leader of a most irksome rebellion that has plagued the kingdom for a generation. He has cost the realm many thousands of ducats and the lives of many of my men."

Allyson looked down at the bunny and laughed out loud.

The king was not amused. "My kingdom is most enlightened, and truly cares about all creatures large and small," he said. "My realm has a judicial system second to none in all the kingdoms of the world. My judges are of the utmost integrity, and excellently trained in all matters before the law. However, because Rudolfo has broken so many of my kingdom's laws I must take the rebel leader to my dungeons. Then my courts will try him justly."

The king's words were smooth, flowing off his tongue as thick cream from a silver pitcher. They had that sweet sound that pulled a sense of trust from deep within, much like the trust Allyson felt with her Gram and Grampa.

The king reached out to take the rabbit, but Allyson moved back a step and said she couldn't give him over to the king.

The king spent the next half hour speaking in such wonderful prose, using such convincing logic and with such deeply felt senti-ments, that Allyson was almost persuaded to turn Rudolfo over to him.

Something in the back of her mind, though, said *danger,* so she said, "No, I will keep him for protection. And would your highness please send your dogs away?"

The king hesitated a moment, and Allyson felt in that brief instant a most unpleasant sensation. The feeling passed, and the king smiled and spoke something to the two dogs, who then trot-ted off back into the forest.

❧   ❧   ❧

The rabbit, who had remained silent through all this, suddenly started to talk, startling Allyson so she almost dropped him. He spoke directly to the king in forceful words, accusing him of most mean and vicious things.

He described the guards of his kingdom, especially Toomer and Jason, as the meanest animals in the realm. They intimidated all animals, took delight as they tortured innocent creatures, and out-right killed those who were declared enemies of the king.

Rudolfo uttered quietly, "My family were all treated in this man-ner. My son and I are the only survivors remaining to lead the creatures."

The king objected to this characterization. Again the silvery words poured out, and again Allyson could feel the pull and power of his eloquence.

Rudolfo didn't blink an eye and countered the king's protesta-tions. He told of numerous atrocities perpetrated by the king's dogs that spanned years, and of how they kept the creatures of the kingdom living in constant fear. Their maltreatment of the citizens knew no bounds, and they relished causing such pain.

The bunny turned to Allyson, describing how his son had taken over the rebellion from him because he was now too old to endure the rigors of the battle. The creatures of the realm loved his son and feared and hated the king and all his mean-spirited kith and kin.

The king scowled and started to protest, but held his tongue. Instead, with honey-dripping words he invited Allyson to come to his castle, meet his supreme judges, talk with his counselors, and hear the people speak. As a measure and token of his trust, he offered to Allyson his own golden ring, the all-powerful symbol of the kingdom.

Allyson reluctantly agreed to visit. She took the ring, but the hair on the back of her neck stood on end. The bunny in her arms stiffened, confirming her sense of the king's deeper intentions. She knew she would have to get back home as soon as possible, and with the rabbit.

⇝　　⇝　　⇝

Since arriving in the king's forest she had not moved very far from her original landing spot, despite all the incidents surrounding the chase of Rudolfo and her protection of him, followed by her lengthy interchange with the king.

She didn't want to make any obvious or suspicious moves, so she tried to look around without appearing to be looking for something.

Out of the corner of her eye, Allyson could see the trunk in the clearing near the edge of the forest, and *she* was standing beside it. Allyson told the king she would follow him to his castle, so he started off into the dark forest with Allyson close behind.

Suddenly Toomer and Jason, who had trotted off earlier, came racing out of the darkness with their fangs bared, lunging at Allyson and Rudolfo. The king had betrayed her trust! There was a flurry of figures and bodies and angry movement, and then the woman was standing between the king and his dogs and their quarry.

She threw her cloak over Allyson and her furry companion, and the king and his henchdogs were forced to shield their eyes as a blinding flash obliterated everything for the briefest of moments. When their vision cleared, the cloaked woman, Allyson, and the rabbit were gone.

Allyson could still see the king, who was furious, and the dogs, who ran in puzzled circles, searching and sniffing. The woman said they were invisible, hidden in the folds of her cloak: "They can't see us." The woman then nodded in the direction of the clearing, and they walked quickly to the trunk.

The woman opened the lid, and Allyson stepped inside with the rabbit and scrunched down, the woman closing the lid after them. The bunny snuggled deeper into Allyson's arms, and when the soft swishing sounds began, it relaxed completely. The sounds seemed to last longer on the return journey, but eventually they slowed and died as they always did.

⅗   ⅗   ⅗

The woman lifted the lid, and the two travelers stepped out and into Allyson's grandparents' attic. Rain still beat on the windows; Allyson could hear the wind howling outside the panes mixing with strains of Verdi.

The woman whispered something into Allyson's ear before turning to step through the surface of the floor-length mirror. Just before her image faded in the silvered glass, she smiled and nodded. Allyson waved, and the woman was gone. Allyson looked

65

around the attic, and then down at the bunny still clutched to her chest. It was a stuffed child's bunny, wearing a green vest—and on its wrist was the king's golden ring...

Land's End

Daphne ran down the dusty road toward the landing, the wind whistling through her hair, her bare legs pumping like pistons.

Her brother, Griff, was coming home for the summer from Auburn University on the launch from Atlanta. He had a layover of two hours before catching the launch, but now it was only a matter of minutes before he would be home.

Mom was at work and wouldn't be able to meet Griff at the docks, and Dad was returning from Atlanta himself but wouldn't be back until late tonight, so Daphne was the family's welcoming committee.

At the crossroads, Daphne cut across the meadow behind the Brands' farmhouse, heading toward the river. The grasses there were waist high and whipped past her as she flew with her feet barely touching the ground.

Her heart was pounding, and her long hair streamed over her shoulders.

She crossed the river near the bottoms, balancing on the old tree trunk that had lain across a section of the river for over two hundred years, some thought.

She slowed to a walk where the path narrowed close by the pond. The air hung heavily around her, and silence spread over the woods. Weaving to avoid a low-hanging branch, Daphne nearly stumbled over a man lying under the tree.

She screamed, jumping back. The man was dressed in ragged clothing and had blood all down his front. He moaned, moving a bit, and Daphne stood back several paces, watching him warily.

He was a smallish man. She called out to him, "Do you need any help?" but the man just tried to move away. Daphne could see that he had lost a lot of blood, most of it staining his shirtfront a dark red.

As Daphne came closer, she could see he was very young. He looked up into Daphne's eyes, and she now saw that he was just a boy, not much older than herself, maybe fourteen or fifteen years old.

His eyes were big, open wide, and filled with fear. He tried to lift himself up to move away while still clutching his stomach, his arms and hands covered in his own blood.

Daphne knelt beside the boy and gently pried his hands away from his body, pulling his shirt open. There were two ugly red wounds in his upper abdomen, still oozing blood. She thought they must be bullet wounds.

Daphne told the boy, "You wait here, and I'll get help," but the boy grabbed her arm, his eyes pleading.

"No, please don't leave me alone!" he cried out, fighting back tears.

Daphne put her hand on his shoulder and said, "I won't leave you."

Tearing off a piece of the boy's shirt, she folded it into a square and placed it tightly against one of the wounds. She then repeated this, pressing a second square in place. The young boy groaned and passed out.

The young boy's head was hot, burning up with fever.

Reaching down, Daphne tore off the bottom of her T-shirt. She knelt at the edge of the pond and dipped it into the fetid waters, wrung it out and took it back to the unconscious boy, placing it on his forehead. She repeated this several times, turning the wet cloth every few minutes.

The boy moaned, eyelids fluttering. He then opened his eyes and tried to focus them.

Daphne did what she could to keep him from moving, but he looked away and attempted to shift his weight.

He moved only slightly, pain shooting through his body. The boy grimaced and clutched at his stomach, then slowly loosened his clenched teeth, sucking in a deep breath.

He was weak from the loss of so much blood.

Daphne asked him his name.

"Billy Joel," this said slowly and barely audibly.

"How did you get shot?" asked Daphne, looking curiously at the boy.

At first, he didn't answer; then he murmured, "Genrul Sherman's men."

Daphne looked down at the boy, her mind racing to comprehend what she had just heard. She sat down next to him and lifted one of the cloth bandages to check his injuries. The wound was only bleeding a little now.

She looked back into the boy's eyes and asked, "Who did this?" The boy closed his eyes and turned his head away.

A sudden crashing sound came through the underbrush near the pond. The boy turned his head, and fear filled his eyes.

He grabbed Daphne's arm and pulled her down hard behind the tree trunk. The effort took its toll, and the boy fell back against the tree, passing into unconsciousness again.

Daphne looked through the branches above her head and watched as two young men came pushing through the brush and along the path toward the pond. They were no more than twenty feet away.

The two men appeared hot and dirty, and were very angry. They carried long rifles. Daphne gasped and covered her mouth with her hand. The two men wore the uniforms of Union soldiers, and their rifles were old muzzleloaders, the kind her grandfather had in his attic.

One man swore under his breath and said, "We gonna catch a farstorm o'hell fum Capt'n James if'n we don't have our prisner!"

The second man bent down and drank deeply from the pond, then coughed and spat out the brackish water. He leaned back against a rock at the pond's edge and nodded agreement, saying, "If'n Capt'n James don't giv us heck, Colonel Thomas surely gonna!"

"Either way, we in a heap 'o trouble for lettin' him git away!"

The men got up, collected their rifles and ran past the two hidden figures, heading along the path toward the road beyond.

Silence returned to the woods, except for the shallow breathing of one unconscious young boy.

Daphne watched his irregular breathing. After a while the boy opened his eyes, but he was too weak and feverish to move more than a little.

Daphne asked, "What did you mean when you said General Sherman's men shot you?"

The boy looked up at Daphne, his half-closed eyes dim and glazed. He moved his mouth and whispered something, but Daphne couldn't hear him. She moved her ear close to his mouth.

He said slowly: "Colonel...Thomas." Then silence, as the effort took a lot out of him. His breathing was shallow and labored. He opened his mouth, then paused. "Captain...James." Again, silence.

Billy coughed, his body tight with pain. He looked into Daphne's eyes, a deep sadness touching his own. He coughed again, then closed his eyes, which frightened Daphne.

Anxiously she spoke his name and he slowly opened his eyes, but she could see that he was no longer focusing them. His breathing grew shallower. Shortly his body relaxed, and he stopped breathing.

⁊ ⁊ ⁊

Daphne touched his cheek, but there was no response. She clasped his hand in hers, but his skin was already cold to the touch. Daphne swallowed back a sob as tears rolled down her face. She pulled his shirt closed over his body and touched her fingers to his lips.

Getting up, she paced back and forth, unsure of her next course of action. She had never been around a dead person before, had never been present when someone died. What was she supposed to do? And what if the two men came back?

Finally she decided she had to go for help. Griff would be waiting at the landing, and she knew if she got to him right away he would know what to do.

Daphne broke several branches off the tree above her head and covered the boy up to his chin. Then, with tears filling her eyes, she raced off in the direction of the landing and her brother.

⁊ ⁊ ⁊

As Daphne ran along the path next to the river, she heard hoof-beats coming up behind her. She stopped and stood off to one side, thinking she would be able ask for help. Her eyes grew big as she watched a huge man dressed in a blue uniform with a shiny sword hanging from his belt ride up on a white horse.

"Good day, miss," said the rider. "I've lost two of my men and can't seem to find them anywhere. Perhaps you've seen them."

The words were spoken politely but urgently, and something in the back of her mind told Daphne to be careful.

"I'm afraid I can't help you," said Daphne. Then, "Pardon me, sir, but are you what I think you are?" she asked, one eyebrow arching in curiosity.

The man laughed and asked, "What do you think I am?"

"A Union officer?" replied Daphne.

The man put his fingers to his hat. "Colonel Nelson Bromwell Thomas at your service, young lady. And who might you be?"

Daphne stiffened slightly upon hearing his name, then cursed herself for having done so.

"Daphne Lynn Petrie, sir," she said. Daphne's subtle move had not gone unnoticed by the colonel, nor had her red eyes, but he made no comment.

He explained that his men had captured a rebel soldier, who'd been found in the nearby town and was thought to be a spy. The colonel added, "I sent my captain, one Burton Windham James, in search of my soldiers, but none of them have been seen for over two days."

"Would your men shoot him if they found him?" asked Daphne innocently.

"Oh, of course not," said the colonel, his face softening, a twinkle in his eyes. "We just want to talk to him."

Daphne said she had seen nothing, knowing this was a huge lie. "I'm on my way to the landing to meet my brother, who's coming in on the launch from Atlanta," she added.

The colonel smiled; then, leaning down with concern in his eyes, he said, "You tell your brother he best mind where he goes today, as

General Sherman and his troops are makin' their way from Atlanta to Savannah not far from here."

Daphne looked into the eyes of the colonel and held his gaze, then thanked him. The colonel looked down at the young girl, and touching his hand to his hat turned his mount north toward the bottoms and galloped off. He did not look back. Daphne turned south and raced like the wind.

Griff was sitting on his duffle bag on the landing when Daphne came running around the corner of the post office. She flew into his arms and almost knocked him over, squeezing him hard as he rumpled her hair and laughed.

After a few moments, Griff noticed that her eyes were red and puffy. "What's wrong, sis?"

Daphne's words came pouring out like a torrent: "I found this young boy who'd been shot an' he died of his wounds, and these two Union soldiers who were angry and in a terrible state came by looking for the boy but I hid him and they missed us. Then a Union officer named Colonel Nelson Thomas rode up looking for Captain Burton James and two soldiers, but I didn't say anything about them, and he rode off up north, and I need you to come help me do something with the dead boy! Please!"

Griff put his hands over Daphne's mouth and said, "Slow down, girl!"

Daphne pulled on his arm and said, "C'mon, we have to hurry. I left the boy's body behind a tree!"

As the two hurried down the street to the edge of town, Griff told her, "I know of Colonel Thomas and Captain James."

Daphne was surprised and shot him a quick sideways glance.

Griff went on: "Both were officers under General William

Tecumseh Sherman, and were party to the terrible destruction the general caused throughout Georgia during his march from Atlanta to the sea."

Griff continued softly: "Colonel Thomas and Captain James were infamous hereabouts, according to legend being the ones responsible for leveling the town in anger. Captain James's men pillaged the bank and burned all the buildings along Main Street to their foundations, while Colonel Thomas set troops about putting the town's church to the torch, reducing it to a pile of smoldering ashes. Eighty-three townspeople died that day!" he finished sadly.

Daphne turned off the dirt road onto the path leading into the woods. She led Griff along the path and through the underbrush to the quiet pond. The air was still heavy and oppressive, and silence filled the woods.

They found the tree where Daphne had left the young boy under a blanket of branches, but found neither the boy's body nor anything of the branches she'd used to cover him.

The leaves on the ground were undisturbed, and appeared to have been in place for some time; there was no sign of any blood on the ground.

Daphne looked around, puzzled and in disbelief.

"Did you have a dream about all this?" asked Griff, but Daphne bristled at the suggestion.

She slumped to her knees beside the tree trunk and, frowning, looked up at her curious and dubious brother.

Daphne ran her hands over the dirt and leaves, her eyes searching the ground. After a moment her fingers touched something hard. She picked it up, and she and Griff examined it closely.

It was a shiny percussion cap, the kind, Griff said, used with muzzle-loading rifles during the Civil War. He was puzzled, as it was pristine and not corroded.

"Sherman's men moved through this area creating havoc. It was likely dropped by one of his men," said Griff.

Daphne didn't believe it for a minute; she knew how it got there under the tree...

The Enchanted Valley

Ulysses had been gone since Saturday, and Calle was worried. Curiosity was his middle name, and being here in the woods provided him an unending source of distractions.

At home he usually spent a lot of his time outdoors, but he stuck close to Calle and was always back in before sundown. Going missing was just not like him. Ulysses was only ten months old, a gift for Calle's seventh birthday.

She picked Ulysses as a name because this kitten was always into everything, reminding her of the voyages of Ulysses and all the troubles and ordeals he fell into. Of the many stories her dad read to her at bedtime or while she did her chores, the story of Ulysses was her favorite.

Her father was an architect who designed houses and buildings and bridges. Calle loved his bridges. He was also a storyteller, and his list of bedtime stories for Calle was lengthy. And he liked to make puns.

Her mother was a research astrophysicist and professor at the university. Calle occasionally sat in the back of the lecture hall, listening to her mother speak about star systems and galaxies, and particularly loved to watch her draw pieces of the night sky on the chalkboard.

It was clear that Calle came by her intelligence and incisive mind through good strong genes, her sense of fun and humor through her attachment to her dad, and her connections and fascination with the universe and the world around her through her mom. She was a blend of sheer childhood delight and wonder, and maturity well beyond her tender age.

Calle loved being out in the woods. She remembered her first summer at the cabin, when her dad caught the granddaddy of all rainbow trout, a major event—she was three and a half.

He held it close for her to see, its tiny round eyes dark pools of unfathomable intelligence, its sides slippery and beautiful in the hues of its namesake, its mouth frightfully opening and closing, gasping in the oxygen-rich but deadly air.

Then her dad said, "That's enough!" and set the fish gently back into the stream and let it go. It hesitated but a moment, then was gone with the flash of its tail fin.

This year, Calle had promised to keep a close eye on Ulysses, especially when they left the cabin. Out in the woods everything was so interesting, and the little cat got easily distracted.

But somehow Ulysses had been too curious and too quick for her, and in one brief moment of Calle's inattention he was gone.

That was two days ago, and Ulysses was still not back. Upset and anxious to find him, Calle set out early one morning before sunup with a satchel containing a piece of cheese, a small wax paper bag of Ritz crackers, and a can of apple juice. She headed for the river, where she thought Ulysses might have gone.

When she arrived at the bluff overlooking the river, she climbed over the edge and onto the narrow path leading to the water. Starting down, it was tight, and she leaned into the cliffside to keep her balance.

Just ten feet from the bottom, Calle's foot slipped on some pebbles, and she tumbled down the remaining portion of the path and onto the sandy bank beside the river.

When the dust settled, but before Calle picked herself up, she checked to see that she was all right. "A few bumps and a scraped knee, but no broken bones," she said out loud to herself. She was sitting spread-legged facing the river.

"You were very lucky," came a high-pitched voice in front of her.

Calle looked up and straight into the dark round pupils of a peregrine falcon perched on a fallen tree on the riverbank. She tried to speak, but no words would come.

"Don't be frightened," said the falcon, "we've been expecting you."

Calle opened her mouth again but still could not bring herself to speak, so deep was her surprise.

The falcon cocked his head to one side, and with both eyes pinning her in place, waited.

"Who are you?" asked Calle when she finally found her voice. "And what do you mean you've been expecting me?"

The falcon begged her pardon: "I am so sorry for being inconsiderate. I am known by the name Scree." He paused, then continued, "I am second in command in the struggle against the Terrible Three who brought darkness to the Enchanted Valley ten winters ago. As for how we knew you were coming, why, Wolf the Oracle told the king you would show up soon."

Scree then dipped his beak in a sign of respect. "Please, come with me. The king has been awaiting your arrival for some time, and he is quite anxious to meet you."

The falcon flew off with Calle following, leading her deep into the woods.

Soon the trees and underbrush became so thick that darkness closed in around her. Calle had great difficulty keeping Scree in sight. Her frustration grew, and she was also starting to feel a bit frightened. Just then, a deep booming voice spoke to her out of the darkness: "You have come just in time."

Calle looked in the direction of the voice, but could only make out the faint silhouette of a figure with large brown eyes that shone out of the darkness. The figure stepped from the shadows, and Calle jumped back, startled, for it was a huge lion with a massive golden-brown mane.

"It is well that you have arrived," said the lion, "for your help is sorely needed."

Calle looked into the eyes of the big cat, and there was a moment of recognition.

"Yes," said the lion, nodding. "In your world you call me by the name Ulysses," but before he could go on, Calle leaped up and threw her arms around his neck.

The lion laughed, a laughter deep and resonant. When Calle let go of his mane and stepped back, he added, "Welcome, little one. It is good to see you. I am glad you are well—Scree told me of your fall at the cliffs."

Then the lion went on, "The creatures in the Enchanted Valley call me by the name of Pyramus, and I am their king."

Scree told Calle the history of how the Terrible Three had arrived in the Enchanted Valley a decade ago, of how they set all the creatures of the valley against one another and brought fear into their midst through acts of evil meanness.

"Their leader goes by the name Slither. He's a python, and the most devilish of the three," said Scree. "He speaks with a quite noticeable lisp, but his command of the spoken word is grand and masterful. That, together with an evil and hypnotic eye, makes him undaunted and deadly to a fault. Few can match the strength of his will, or stand firm against the power of his tongue."

Scree paused to preen at his feathers, then continued, "Akhbar Khan, the Siberian tiger, has more brute force than persuasion. Through intimidation accentuated with rippling muscles and sharp claws, he serves as Slither's right-paw henchman. He's not averse to strong-paw tactics, and is most pleased when others are ill at ease in his presence, for this is in part his intent when he walks among them."

The falcon clacked his beak three times. "Finally, Jackal, the hyena, is the last and perhaps most dangerous of the three, being the one seemingly the least in control of his own mind. Tragedy is his mirth, misfortune his humor, and calamity his delight. Actually, Slither is never quite certain if Jackal will remain under any degree of self-control. At any moment he might explode in a savage fit of unbridled violence."

Now Scree bowed his proud head. "However, that uncertainty suits Slither's intentions well, for he considers it a calculated uncertainty to keep the creatures and his enemies constantly off balance and off their guard."

It was becoming clear to Calle the presence of the unholy three was a tremendous weight on the entire Enchanted Valley. As the years wore on under their influence, the times would grow darker and the creatures more vulnerable.

Scree went on, "The day that Pyramus came to the Enchanted Valley, the creatures were once again with hope. He was strong, but not without fear, for he knew the value of caution.

"Slither's evil eye held no sway with Pyramus and his steely eyes," said Scree, "and Akhbar Khan was no match for Pyramus's powerful size and sharp claws. Only Jackal, with his unbalanced mind firmly ensconced in the netherworld, was undaunted by Pyramus's arrival, proving to be a thorn in the latter's paw and a continuing pall over the valley."

"The wisdom of the ancients, passed down to us by Wolf the Oracle, told us of the day a fair young maiden would come to deliver the valley from evil," said Pyramus, looking directly into Calle's eyes. There was a moment of silence as Calle felt all attention turned upon her.

Finally, a nervous and somewhat puzzled Calle asked, "But, what can I do? I am only a little girl!"

"You are very strong, in ways other than Akhbar Khan, and wise in means that Slither does not comprehend. You will know when you face the one named Jackal what you must do," replied Pyramus.

⸺　　⸺　　⸺

Thus it was that on the next day at high noon, at the base of the bluffs alongside the river, Calle sat on a rock and waited alone.

"What if I don't do the right thing?" she muttered to herself. "What if I make a mistake?" again, half to herself.

"Why, then you lose," came a sneering whispered reply from behind her.

Calle spun around and found herself looking directly into the cold amber eyes of Jackal, the hyena.

Jackal chuckled, muttering things under his breath that Calle didn't understand.

His voice had sharp edges, and he spoke so rapidly Calle recognized only a few of his angry words.

The rest were unintelligible ravings.

Jackal grew increasingly agitated. His words came more rapidly, and his eyes darted back and forth. He paced, his cold amber gaze turning a fiery red.

Calle was amazed at her own calmness in the face of Jackal's rantings. Instinctively, without a thought for safety, she reached out a hand and gently touched his nose. Calle then leaned over, and resting one arm around his shoulder brushed her lips against his high cheekbone.

Suddenly there was a momentary and blinding flash of light. After that, everything went black.

Calle heard her name called, though she heard it only faintly and from afar. She opened her eyes and found her father bending over her.

"You must have fallen down the cliff and bumped your head," he said. "Are you okay?"

Calle sat up and looked around her. Ulysses was there, and jumped up on her lap and licked her hand.

Years later Calle would recall how she explained it to her father on that day: "First I met Scree, who led me deep into the Enchanted Valley, and there was Jackal the hyena, the most dangerous of them all, and Ulysses was really Pyramus, who was king over all the creatures."

She remembered how her father had smiled and felt her forehead, Ulysses jumping up to lick her cheek—and she would swear in the bright sunlight that he looked deep into her eyes and winked…

Dreamscape

Julie lay under a light cotton sheet watching the shadows dance across the ceiling of her room. The candle in its holder sat on the nightstand, and a slight breeze coming in through the open window caused the flame to flicker, casting sinuous forms of light and dark above.

The sun had set amid gathering thunderheads, the golden tinge around the edges of the clouds on the horizon giving the western sky a warm glow. Then, all was darkness as the storm moved in off the ocean. It was now past 10 o'clock, and a warm rain was falling outside. Julie felt restless, and not a bit sleepy.

❧　　❧　　❧

Dr. George Neville, Julie's dad, was the lead astronomer, though the youngest by far, of the team of veteran sky watchers at the Golden Hinde Observatory just outside Melbourne.

The transmissions from the Gemini probe were expected to begin shortly after midnight tonight, the culmination of the second stage in a ten-year mission to gather information from the far reaches of the solar system.

Set in synchronous orbit on the plane of the planet Neptune were two enormous x-ray–enhanced radio telescopes, their orbits and angles of scan controlled by the Gemini team at control central.

Each of the two orbiting dishes spanned twenty meters, edge to edge, and both were linked through some of the most advanced and sophisticated computers in existence, much of it commissioned through special arrangements with the military.

The ten-year mission of the Gemini Project was to seek out and identify a mysterious force beyond the orbit of the eighth planet, Styx, the effects of which were influencing the orbits of all the outer planets. These transmissions from Gemini were eagerly awaited by the worldwide astronomical community.

⇝   ⇝   ⇝

Julie watched with fascination as shadows played across the ceiling of her attic bedroom. They were matched by similar patterns of light and dark that moved across the fields of her mind. She lay in the semi-darkness, the warm breeze washing over her, the sounds of the rain-filled night playing outside her window.

Then, as had happened on several occasions before, a woman in a flowing garment appeared out of the shadows in the corner near the window and stood beside her bed. She smiled down at Julie and held her gaze with deep blue eyes. She held out her hand. Julie grasped it, rose from her bed, and walked with the woman over to the window overlooking the backyard.

Outside, rain pelted the familiar oak tree, its broadly spread limbs unbending under the added weight.

The two sat down on the window seat, pulled their knees up under their chins, and wrapped the heavy comforter around their shoulders.

The night sounds died away, the light from the candle on the nightstand dimmed, and the room's walls swirled in a silent vortex around the two. Julie closed her eyelids over deep blue eyes. Then there was darkness, and the absence of all sound.

≈　　≈　　≈

Dr. Neville stood with the team's technical advisory group behind a technician at the main monitor. On the large green screen, and over the system's speakers, there was the usual interference, the crackling intergalactic white noise that was always present. Added to this were the occasional blips and beeps as the technician keyed instructions at the console.

Suddenly, the quiet murmurings in the control room and the background noise of the universe were broken by the distinct sound that all knew was the initial message from Gemini.

Computers around the control room whirred to life, their lights blinking in sympathetic union with the two distant travelers, and the first stages of transmission began. Team members stopped and turned to the monitors to watch the incoming message.

≈　　≈　　≈

Julie felt a slight chill as her world went dark. Time seemed to stop. She snuggled against the woman and buried herself in the satin blanket. After what seemed an age, the ringing in her ears stopped, and she felt a tingling sensation all over. She could feel the temperature around her dropping and could see a cold blue-grey light through her half-closed eyelids.

Her traveling companion was still there, warm, supple, and secure. Julie tried to move but felt no response from her body. In fact, she couldn't feel her body at all. The woman was there, but then, not.

In the far reaches of her mind, she heard the woman speak, and was baffled because it seemed she was hearing from inside where her head should be.

"Yes, you are hearing me with your mind," said the woman. "Here we have no bodies."

Julie looked around her, but there was only darkness. The woman instructed her to listen with her mind, and to visualize with her mind; it would take practice.

After a while, Julie could see lights around her, lights of different colors and intensities. The woman said the lights were life forms from another place in the galaxy, and their colors told who they were.

* * *

Monitors came to life, and vast fields of numbers streamed across the screens. The Gemini team watched in rapt wonder as the twin satellites transmitted their coded signals. The main computer's program worked the immense body of numbers and began the process of deciphering their encoded meaning.

At Dr. Neville's direction, the technician keyed in the codes accessing the preliminary readings, and a picture slowly began to form on the master screen.

To everyone's amazement except for Dr. Neville, there were shadings of grey and light and shadow, and vast areas in between devoid of all matter.

The technician keyed in another set of instructions, and another. The forms on the screen changed, taking on more definition, the contrast increasing.

The technician keyed in a fourth instruction, and the screen transformed into a beautiful visual of shapes and forms of light and dark.

Dr. Neville watched as spiral arms turned and moved sinuously though ever so slowly across the screen. Growing pinpoints of light shone out of the vast void of space between gaseous clouds of matter, and their colors gradually shifted from blue to blue-grey, and back to blue again.

❧   ❧   ❧

Julie felt the presence of a dark light form nearby. She sensed its presence more than anything else. Despite radiating a form of light, it lacked any warmth at all, and Julie shivered.

There was also a dull lavender light form that trailed the darker being, almost as though it was a tail trailing a comet.

The lavender light gave Julie a terrible feeling, one of emptiness, like nothing she was familiar with back home.

Then, Julie sensed yet a third light form—this one was a greyish brown light that made her blood run cold and clouded her mind. It was incongruous to call it light because its form was almost invisible. Like the other forms, it gave Julie a bad feeling inside.

The dark light form moved around Julie and her companion. It spoke in words that felt at once velvety and smooth, yet which stirred pain in the back reaches of Julie's mind. Julie was confused. The words felt good, as of wholeness and sunshine. "But why does it hurt so to hear them?" asked Julie.

The woman spoke softly, but with a power that startled Julie. She challenged the dark light form, and countered its pain, its distress, its darkness. Julie felt warmth returning, and she relaxed.

❧   ❧   ❧

Dr. Neville sensed that something was wrong with the vast parade of numbers appearing in the computer's visual memory matrix, but couldn't put his finger on the problem.

His assistant, Dr. Brigitte Najinski, pointed out a series of numbers she thought affected some of the shadow areas in the image on screen, and suggested that they were reciprocals and the computer had incorrectly calculated them.

Dr. Najinski keyed in a complex series of instructions and waited. The picture changed, but only in subtle ways.

Dr. Neville watched with fascination. The light areas grew dimmer, as several dark areas seemed to draw light from them.

Dr. Neville said, "I believe what we're observing is energy transformation accompanying the genesis of a star. It seems this phenomenon is not occurring anywhere near our solar system, but elsewhere in a distant galaxy, and through some unique effect this amazing event is being witnessed in our galactic neighborhood."

≥　≥　≥

The lavender light form hissed at the woman, and Julie cringed. The woman looked directly into the brightest area of light and stared it down.

The lavender light seemed to squirm, its intensity alternately rising and falling. It withdrew in haste behind the dark light form.

The greyish brown light then moved rhythmically around the two companions. Its form was deceptively attractive, but the woman shielded Julie from it and told her not to look directly at it.

Julie could feel the penetrating cold, which also made her drowsy. The woman generated her own powerful light that countered the negative greyish brown light. Her side by Julie glowed with warmth while the other, facing the dimmer light, lost temperature and grew colder.

The woman urged Julie to fight the dimming lights, to counter their drawing of warmth and energy from her with the light within herself.

Dr. Najinski tweaked the keyboard once again with her magical fingers. The computer hummed, and the forms on screen moved in their subtle dance of light and dark. Gradually, the gaseous areas of light swirled and coalesced into brighter forms, and eventually into star masses surrounded by vast areas the blackness of midnight.

As the screen stopped its dancing, there appeared a twin energy source, surrounded by three lesser forms. Energy passed back and forth between the twin energy points and the three satellites, and the brightness of the twins waxed and waned, but gradually grew. With each cycle of energy transfer and transformation, the double source increased in power, and the three lesser gave up their energies, their lights dimming.

Julie felt her mind begin to clear, her projected self warming amidst the various light forms that moved around her.

The woman drew her circle of light around Julie, and this added to the growing warmth she felt. The lights of the lesser and darker light forms dimmed even more, and Julie could feel memory traces of pain drop away and diminish.

The darkness split, and midnight spilled out onto the landscape of the universe, running down jagged mountainsides into valleys, along riverbeds, and into the western galaxies.

The Gemini team watched as the screen grew alternately brighter and darker, eventually ending with a portrait of light forms heretofore unobserved—a double star, with three dark planets circling in synchronous orbits, each trailing a dark shadow of a tail. The double star glowed blue shading into blue-grey, then back into blue.

Julie opened her eyes. The warm night breeze gently moved the candle flame, casting shadows across the meadows of her mind and onto the ceiling...

The Edge of Darkness

A strong wind blew down out of the mountain pass from the north, bringing a brisk chill to the morning.

A lone figure stood beside a magnificent stallion on the crest of a hill overlooking the lush green valley. He was dressed in armor the color of onyx, a lavender plume adorning his helmet, his visor of burnished gold, a long and a short sword strapped at his side. His steed was a full eighteen hands tall at the shoulders, his coat a shiny black that matched his rider.

The two stood in the shadows of an ancient oak as the rider surveyed the countryside ahead.

Suddenly, there was a rush of air and the flapping of wings, and a powerful gyrfalcon swooped down out of the sky and came to perch on the outstretched and gloved fist of the dark rider.

"Hmmm," murmured the Black Knight.

"Hmmm," added his steed ShadowFax.

"What say you?" asked the Black Knight of the falcon. "Is it clear through the valley?"

"It is clear," said Rogue, preening himself, "and very quiet."

"What of Twilight?" asked the Black Knight.

"I saw no signs of his comings or goings," replied Rogue, "but he is there—I felt his presence."

"Good," said the Black Knight.

ShadowFax stamped his right forehoof, and the muscles across his neck rippled as he champed at his bit. "I don't like it, Maq," he whispered. "Something is afoot."

Rogue added that he had heard nothing unusual, nor had he seen anything out of the ordinary as he flew his course over the valley.

The Black Knight was thoughtful as he looked beyond the river. "I hold your same caution, ShadowFax," he said to his trusty companion, "but I don't believe he has returned."

"Perhaps, but clearly there is fear across the realm," said Rogue.

The Black Knight nodded, adding there was just cause to be fearful. Count Tanner, the Count of Darkness, had engaged the services of the evil wizard Haliburton to cast spells over much of the western reaches. Dark days indeed face the realm of King Fissure of Embaline.

Maq the Knight had been summoned by King Fissure on a matter of dire urgency—his daughter, Princess Tara, had been kidnapped by Count Tanner, and was being held captive deep in the Sanguine Mountains far to the north.

~ ~ ~

The gateway to the dark mountains was guarded by a fierce dragon, whose keeper was known merely as Jhae the Gnome.

The dragon was said to possess terrible powers, preying especially on the souls of innocents. Storm clouds hung in the skies, dark with foreboding, wherever the dragon mind his keeper went.

Jhae the Gnome had no heart, and his disposition was darker than the shadow side of the moon.

King Fissure feared for the soul of his daughter, and with just cause. Her tender age of thirteen gave him no end of worry.

The Black Knight thrust out his fist, and Rogue spread his wings and lifted easily into the morning air.

"Find Twilight, stay, and come at my bidding," called out the Black Knight.

Rogue circled thrice, and wheeling, flew like the wind out over the valley.

The Black Knight mounted ShadowFax, and the two started down into the peaceful-looking valley.

The winding trail led through open meadows and past stands of trees, but the travelers encountered no one along the way.

They crossed the river and passed ancient homes along the river's edge, and still they saw no one.

The Black Knight took note, but it was ShadowFax who commented, "Dark forces are present; I fear he has returned."

"Hmmm," said the Black Knight.

ShadowFax trotted past fields of grain, following the road which led to the castle. A palpable silence hung heavily on the air.

The two travelers approached and stopped in front of the castle moat. Calling out, the Black Knight asked entrance. Silence. The Black Knight called out a second time, but still there was only silence.

ShadowFax snorted and stamped his hoof, the hoofbeat resounding off the high stone walls. The Black Knight could feel his friend tense his muscles beneath him as they both surveyed the castle and its surroundings.

The Black Knight waited; then, there came a response. From the towering turret beside the massive gate, through a window slit hiding the speaker, came a whispered welcome.

Then, with the creaking of ancient chains and a low rumble, the drawbridge slowly swung down, dropping into place. ShadowFax pranced across and through the iron gate, his hoofbeats echoing off the hardened wood of the bridge.

The Black Knight surveyed the courtyard from astride ShadowFax. Out of the corner of his eye he caught movement, and turning beheld the stately figure of a man standing at the railing of a balcony. The man nodded and disappeared through velvet curtains.

The Black Knight dismounted and walked up the steps into the castle. There he was met by the same man, who led him through long cold corridors to a study high in the northern wing. There he asked the Black Knight to wait.

The Black Knight nodded, and as the man left the room removed his helmet. He walked to the window overlooking the outer moat and gazed past the distant foothills to the sinister mountains beyond.

⚯　⚯　⚯

In a narrow pass, gateway to the Sanguine Mountains, the daemon dragon stood guard with his keeper. There the Princess Tara was held, and the Black Knight whispered a prayer for her well-being until his arrival.

The Black Knight gave no sign of hearing King Fissure enter the room behind him, but before the king could speak he said, "I am here at your command."

King Fissure was startled, then gathering himself said, "My daughter is held in a dark cave beyond those mountains. Return her safely, and whatever you ask is yours."

The Black Knight turned and looked into the eyes of the king. "I will do what I can," he said, a cold fire burning behind his hazel eyes.

"What aid do you need on your quest?" asked the king.

"I have naught but two ancient swords, a crossbow, my trusty steed, and the presence of two spirits of the night world. I need nothing else," said the Black Knight. "Until my return," he whispered.

And with that, he turned and left the king looking out over his kingdom to the northern horizon beyond. The king watched as the Black Knight mounted his horse in the courtyard, and with a salute of his gloved fist rode out the gate, across the moat, and toward the gateway to the misty Sanguine Mountains.

ShadowFax set a steady pace, and the countryside and time passed in due course. Then the Black Knight's sharp eyes caught a dark speck against the clouds above a distant ridge. He brought it to ShadowFax's attention.

"I have been observing it for the past half hour," said ShadowFax. "Rogue is on the wing."

The two moved silently along, watching the dark wheeling speck grow as they approached the foothills.

"Jhae the Gnome will know of our approach," said ShadowFax, picking up his pace slightly.

"He knew of it the moment we left the castle," said the Black Knight.

"Hmmm," said ShadowFax, "that accounts for the gathering storm clouds over the pass."

The sun had long passed its zenith and was on its westering journey to the horizon when the two travelers came to a narrow hanging bridge over the Rhue Gorge, the northernmost boundary of the realm of King Fissure.

ShadowFax started across the bridge. As they approached the

halfway mark, a lone dark figure moved out of the shadows on the far side, taking a place near the stanchion of the bridge.

The figure raised a twin-bladed ax and took one full swing at the massive hemp ropes of the bridge, sending a sickening vibration along the wooden causeway and under the feet of horse and rider.

Before the figure could raise the ax for a second blow, and before the Black Knight could align a bolt in his crossbow, a winged creature swooped out of the darkening skies and with one swift movement, slashed at the figure wielding the ax.

The dark figure recoiled. Turning in one deft movement, he aimed the ax at Rogue's breast. In mid-swing, a blur of blue-grey leaped out of the shadows and grasped the burly assailant by the throat.

The struggle was brief, followed by silence. ShadowFax stamped on the bridge, sending a shudder back along the causeway.

The Black Knight spurred ShadowFax on, and reaching the cliffs found Rogue perching on the massive hemp ties of the bridge alongside the fallen figure. Next to Rogue sat a great grey northern wolf.

"Greetings, Twilight," said the Black Knight. "You timed your arrival quite nicely."

"We have watched you since you left the castle," replied Twilight.

"As has Jhae the Gnome," interjected Rogue. "We'd best get out of the light, lest his eyes in the wilderness catch further glimpses of our ragged band."

⸙   ⸙   ⸙

Once in the shadows of the cliffs beyond the gorge, Rogue reported that Jhae the Gnome was close by, the assailant being his point-guard, which meant that the dragon was not far off either.

Twilight said he had picked up the dragon's scent less than one kilometer to the northeast, and it was fresh.

Rogue added that he had seen neither, a tribute to their powers, but he, too, sensed their presence.

"How far to the lair of the dragon where the princess is held?" asked the Black Knight.

"Two leagues beyond the pass, and the way difficult," responded Rogue. The Black Knight nodded. As the sun set and shadows deepened, the Sanguine Mountains taking on the mantle of the realm of darkness, the band of four moved cautiously in a direct line north.

Coming around a corner of a low-hanging rock, Twilight stiffened momentarily, but with lightning speed lunged forward.

Rogue swept down with talons bared, and together the stalwart pair cornered another of Jhae's forward guards.

ShadowFax placed his hoof on the foot of the snarling guard and looked him squarely in the eyes.

The Black Knight asked his name, then in a moment of recognition whispered, "You are the one known as Jhae the Gnome."

The figure struggled, but ShadowFax's hoof firmly pinned him to the ground. The gnome looked into the dark brown eyes of his captor.

"The dragon is near, and you are all but dead!"

Twilight snarled near the gnome's ear, his warm breath raising the hair on the back of the captive's neck. Beads of sweat formed on Jhae's brow, and a trickle ran down his back.

Then, a low rumble was heard, perhaps initially only felt, and the ground began to move.

Rogue lifted swiftly into the night air, and Twilight slipped into the surrounding darkness. ShadowFax kept his captive's foot pinned to the ground as the rumbling and shaking increased.

The Black Knight strung a bolt to his crossbow, and drawing his long sword moved out of the shadows into the clearing.

Beyond the curtain of darkness, the Black Knight could see a fiery light approaching in his direction. He could hear the underbrush crumble under the weight of some mighty creature, and brush fires sprang up where the creature passed.

Suddenly, the beast was there in front of the Black Knight, towering twenty feet above him, all muscle and teeth, breathing blue-green fires out of both nostrils.

Twilight appeared out of the darkness from the left and lunged at the creature's midsection. Rogue swooped out of the midnight heavens and ripped at the dragon's fierce eyes.

As the dragon feigned to its left, the Black Knight let fly a single bolt, true to his aim, striking the dragon squarely between the eyes, crushing its skull.

The dragon stood for a moment, its eyes disbelieving, and then with a low moan fell like ancient timber in the forest, taking a full dozen trees down with him.

Then, there was silence.

   ≯ ≯ ≯

Jhae the Gnome screamed and threw himself against ShadowFax's leg, writhing in anger. ShadowFax increased the pressure on the captive's foot, adding to his pain.

The Black Knight directed the gnome to lead the way to the hidden cave wherein Princess Tara was held. The gnome scowled and spat on the ground, saying, "The way is hidden. You shall never discover it in time!"

ShadowFax applied the full weight of his eighty-six stones to the gnome's foot, raising the price of his refusal. The gnome screamed and slipped into unconsciousness.

The Black Knight grabbed him by the scruff of the neck, and lifting him off the ground held him close to his face.

As the gnome opened his eyes, he found himself looking down the bolt of the Black Knight's crossbow. His eyes widened, the barbed black arrowhead pricking his forehead, drawing blood.

"The cave is behind a floating rock that moves on command," stammered the gnome. "It is at the end of Sorrow Canyon, north of the Dark Crystal River."

"Take us to her," whispered the Black Knight through set teeth, setting the gnome down.

The moon had traveled but a quarter of the night sky by the time the band arrived in front of the hillside and approached the cave.

The Black Knight prodded the gnome, and Jhae stumbled forward. He looked back at the Black Knight, who held his gaze with steel-hard eyes.

"Ixtyl marshtyg," whispered the gnome before the massive stone. Nothing.

The Black Knight prodded him again, but before he could repeat the words the stone moved forward, then slid to the side with nary a sound.

The Black Knight removed his helmet and stepped to the mouth of the cave. As his eyes became accustomed to the murkiness within, he sensed a presence off to one side. There, cowering in the darkness, was Princess Tara.

"Be still," he whispered, his voice soft. "Are you well?" he asked.

"I am well," came her wavering reply. "Who are you?"

"I am one sent by your father to return you home," said the Black Knight. "Are you able to travel?"

"I am," she answered. Princess Tara held the arm of the Black Knight as the two emerged into the growing light of morning. There, Jhae the Gnome cowered and whimpered under the watchful eyes of ShadowFax.

The Black Knight nodded, and ShadowFax stepped back. The Black Knight pointed to the east: "Go and n'er darken the realm of King Fissure again, lest you forfeit your life."

And with that Jhae the Gnome scampered into the underbrush, muttering under his breath.

⤳   ⤳   ⤳

The Black Knight lifted the princess onto ShadowFax in front of him, and thus they began the return journey. Rogue circled above, maintaining a watchful eye, as Twilight slipped into the shadow side of daylight; he, too, kept watch.

Princess Tara nestled between the Black Knight's arms and rested easy as the countryside and time passed in due course.

Toward dusk, as eventide settled over the land, they approached the hanging bridge above the Rhue Gorge, and as the setting sun touched the mountain pass with fingers of gold and amber, Princess Tara caught a glimpse through the pass of the Valley of Embaline— she was home...

—With apologies to J.R.R. Tolkien

Fall of the House of ThunderBane

A light snow blanketed the hillsides across the deep valley, glaciers gracing the ancient and high ridges beyond. A full midnight moon shone over the land, casting a silvery blue over all the realm.

The evening was still, with nary a whisper of wind, and a sense of expectancy hung in the crisp night air.

Over the past fortnight rumors of war had circulated widely, and reports on movements of the mighty armies of the Dark Lord, MaleProp, passed the lips of travelers coming from beyond the Tranquility Mountains.

Two figures sat huddled under a thin blanket, looking out across the quiet valley of the House of Lord ThunderBane. They leaned against a large granite outcropping and were warmed by its residual heat from the previous day's sun.

"It is very cold," said the smaller figure.

"Umhmm," said his companion, not moving his eyes from the peaceful scene below.

"We should get you inside," said the smaller one, "else your cough returns."

"Thank you, my friend," said his companion. "It will not be much longer." He paused for a moment, deep in thought, before continuing quietly, "There is one below who awaits us. Once we meet, the time for needed rest will finally be near."

The friend could see his companion shivering under the blanket, but his stubbornness wouldn't allow him to acknowledge this.

"How will you know the one?" asked the friend.

"I am not certain," said his master. "There will be a sign, I think."

Hahr LeQuinn pulled the blanket tighter around himself and his friend. PonteFane crouched closer to provide some added warmth for his master, his forepaws resting comfortably under his chin.

As the two continued their watch, the moon slid behind the mountains to the west and beyond the horizon, while the darkness above the mountains to the east mellowed into the lightness present just before dawn.

"There is much fear in the land," murmured PonteFane, his eyes noting movement as the marketplace began to stir, herders guiding their sheep along the road leading to the meadows and into the hills beyond the village.

"Since the death of my dear friend, Lord ThunderBane, his son, the blundering and deceitful Lord Popynjhay, has laid a heavy hand upon the people," said Hahr LeQuinn softly.

"Yes, and Captain Asholthom of the Royal Guard carries out this reign of terror over his own people in the name of Lord ThunderBane!" added PonteFane, his voice hard.

The two sat a while longer, observing the awakening of the village.

Then, as the sun's first rays lit the hills beyond with touches of gold, Hahr LeQuinn rose and gathered up the blanket, folding it neatly into a compact bundle which he tied with a short piece of hemp.

PonteFane sniffed at the air. Checking the area one last time, he joined his friend as together they moved down the trail toward the village.

☿ ☿ ☿

Haliburton, High Wizard and advisor to His Highness, entered the king's bedroom softly. Leaning over the sleeping king, he touched his shoulder and said, "It is morning, Your Majesty." His voice was high-pitched and rasping, with a tentative undertone.

Again: "It is morning, Lord Popynjhay. It is time."

The king stirred, and opening one eye growled, "Dolt! It is still dark, and the cock has not crowed even once!"

"Aye, 'tis true. But you asked to be awakened before the sun crested the eastern reaches—it is already past that time," whined the wizard.

"Umm, so I did," mumbled Lord Popynjhay, and he staggered out of bed to proceed with his morning toilet and cleansing.

Haliburton nervously paced the hallway outside the king's chambers, muttering to himself: "Oh, me! Oh, my! Oh, oh, oh!"

His eyes darted here and there, perspiration rolling down his neck and back in spite of the damp and coldness inside the castle.

The king is taking too long, thought Haliburton. *This will not do. When he arrives late for this morning's council of war, I will surely receive the brunt of His Majesty's ire.*

On the other hand, it would not do to hurry Lord Popynjhay, for that, too, would incur the wrath of the king of all Transylvania.

Haliburton was caught on the horns of a dilemma, a situation not unfamiliar across the realm when it came to pleasing the king.

Just then, the captain of the king's Royal Guard approached.

"Why isn't the king in the council chambers?" asked Asholthom with a wry smile on his lips and an edge to his tongue. "Did you sleep beyond the appointed hour?"

Haliburton shot him an angry glance, and peering down his aquiline nose quipped, "You'd best tend to your own duties, Asholthom. I understand not all the lords of the realm received their summons in due time for the council, and His Lordship will not be pleased!"

The two fired angry looks back and forth.

"Yes, and no thanks to you, traitor of the people!"

Asholthom sneered and said, "I understand your people impeded the delivery of the call to the lords."

"Untrue, my deceitful friend," shot back the wizard, his voice cracking as it rose.

Just then Lord Popynjhay appeared at the doorway of his bed-chambers, anger boiling behind his amber-green eyes.

Asholthom snapped to attention and raised his fist in salute. Haliburton whimpered audibly and stood as much at attention as his frail body and more frail character permitted. His shoulders slumped pitifully.

"Come, we are late for the council of war!" And with that, the king stormed through the hallways, up the stairs to the western wing, and into the royal council chambers.

❧   ❧   ❧

Approaching the village square, Hahr LeQuinn and PonteFane found a bustling crowd attending to the preparations of the village at the break of morn. PonteFane spied a young girl near the fish vendor throwing pebbles against the sidewall of the stables, and the two approached her.

She was humming a melody that sounded vaguely familiar, yet one with an ancient timbre.

Hahr LeQuinn asked her pardon for interrupting her play, introducing himself and his traveling companion, PonteFane. Her hazel eyes lit up upon seeing PonteFane, and reaching out she patted his nose.

"I am pleased to meet you," said the young girl with a curtsy. "I am called by the name Justyne, daughter and heir to the throne of Lord Tarsynian of the House of Vespuryn in the west."

"I am happy to make your acquaintance," said PonteFane. And, turning to Hahr LeQuinn, he whispered, "She is the one."

⅏   ⅏   ⅏

The lords of the realm had been called together for the first council of war since one was called before the seven-day War of Liberation.

Lord Tarsynian, of House Vespuryn to the west, sat near the western point around the table. He was accompanied by Duryn, his chief counsel and advisor.

Lord Marlborhis, of House Tessuryle in the north, sat to his left around the circle, but to the right of the North Star marking the place at table for the king.

Then sat Lord Mahrbury, son and heir to House Tremayne, also in the north, and next to him Lord Lindershaft of House Fuhrynn, the tiniest realm (though most fierce by reputation) in the east.

The next seat was empty, a silver candlesnuffer resting on the place marker there. Here the Lord Taszhmynn, recent heir to House Valshunne of the eastern region, would sit upon his arrival.

The final chair was that of Lord Sheridan, long the respected overseer of the great southern reaches and head of House Shalimar. His place at council, too, was marked with a silver candlesnuffer.

The gathered lords spoke in hushed tones, their voices calm though controlled. As Lord Popynjhay entered the vaulted chambers, the men stopped their speech, rising as he took his place at the table.

The king surveyed his gathered Council of Lords and motioned with his hand. Asholthom and Haliburton entered the room and took their places behind the king, just outside the Circle of Lords.

Lord Popynjhay began by noting the absence and presumed tardiness of Lords Taszhmynn and Sheridan, a fact he would not countenance. There was a slight edge in his voice.

"Your Highness," interjected Lord Tarsynian firmly, "your summons was just received this morning. I trust that the tardiness of Lords Taszhmynn and Sheridan is due to the distance of their travels rather than any slight on their part of you."

"Perhaps!" replied Lord Popynjhay, still irritated.

Turning to the Council of Lords, he said, "The march of Lord MaleProp across the southern regions distresses me! Tell me, how is it this aged buffoon is permitted such freedom within the realm of the House of Lord ThunderBane?"

"With all due respect, Lord Popynjhay, the Lord MaleProp was never seen by your father as any kind of threat to the realm. This was but one symbol of the pact of cooperation between your father and the realms beyond the Tranquility Mountains," said Lord Tarsynian.

"My father was a fool!" bellowed Lord Popynjhay, cutting Lord Tarsynian off.

A murmur rippled around the Circle of Lords at the king's comment, and not a few were distressed at this maligning of their beloved friend and mentor.

He had not been dead but ten months, and the leadership of his son left much to be desired.

This is going to be a very long day, thought Lord Tarsynian to himself.

"What brings you to our fair land?" asked Justyne eagerly. "Are you to attend the Council of Lords? My father is," she added proudly.

Hahr LeQuinn laughed deeply, though it caused him pain in his chest. This was not lost on PonteFane, who rubbed gently against his master's leg.

"Yes, although we are come for another matter."

Hahr LeQuinn took one of Justyne's hands, and with his other under her chin raised her eyes to meet his.

"We have come to make you an offer you cannot refuse," he said, with a twinkle of mischief in his voice.

"What do you mean?" asked Justyne, her curiosity now aroused.

"Ah, all in good time," replied Hahr LeQuinn with a smile on his lips, the twinkle now in his eyes.

PonteFane asked, "Do you remember your mother?"

Justyne shot him a quick glance, and her eyes closed slightly. "Why do you ask?" she queried the wolf.

PonteFane persisted, "What do you remember of her?"

Justyne hesitated for a moment. Then tears gathered in the corners of her eyes, and she caught her breath.

"My memories are faint, and with little remembered feeling," she answered. "She died when I was still a child. Again, why do you ask?"

"Ah, well, your mother was a fine woman, Justyne," said Hahr LeQuinn. "PonteFane recalls her with great fondness, and a certain gratitude." His eyes met PonteFane's as he spoke, and there was a moment of shared recollection.

PonteFane cleared his throat. "I was at death's doorstep, shot with the bolt of a crossbow, the result of a royal hunt hosted by one Lord Popynjhay.

"Your mother, the daughter of Lord MaleProp from beyond the Tranquility Mountains, was present that day, the guest of Lord ThunderBane. It was then that your mother met Lord Tarsynian, and soon after that they were betrothed—but that is a story of wonderment for yet another time."

PonteFane then continued, "During the hunt I was tracked with great skill, and my attempts to escape danger were cut short at every turn. When at last I was cornered, I attempted one final time to flee, but was shot by one of the hunting party. As I lay near death, your mother, Lady AmberLyn, stood over my body and would not let the death blow be struck, much to the chagrin of Lord Popynjhay and many in the party."

PonteFane sighed, and his eyes held those of Justyne a brief moment.

Hahr LeQuinn spoke softly, adding, "Hidden in the annals of time both in this realm and that of Lord MaleProp is that your father, Lord Tarsynian, is the secret issue of Lord ThunderBane and a woman of mystery in the western reaches, one who remains in the shadows to this day. Thus, your father is not only the son of the revered father of this realm, but elder brother of Lord Popynjhay."

Justyne's eyes closed slightly as the weight of this revelation settled on her mind.

Hahr LeQuinn continued, "The kingdoms of Lord MaleProp and Lord ThunderBane are therefore linked by blood, and the twisting of this by Lord Popynjhay is more dangerous for the realm than the supposed evil intent of Lord MaleProp, your grandfather."

Justyne's eyes posed the question, but before it could be asked Hahr LeQuinn responded, "I was chief counsel to your shadow grandmother, but due to ill health was forced to retire from her service. For reasons known only to Lord ThunderBane, he maintained the secrecy of his son, your father, and what his union with the daughter of Lord MaleProp meant for the two realms. And so it remains until this day."

He paused, searching the eyes of his young listener for understanding.

Justyne smiled, and nodding said, "I have known there was something in the way Lord ThunderBane watched me over the years. His eyes were deep and expressed things I did not understand, until your words just now."

And it came to pass that Justyne appeared before the Council of Lords, to the pleasant surprise of the gathered lords excluding Lord Popynjhay and his cronies. The link between the families of Lord ThunderBane and Lord MaleProp came to light, and Lord Tarsynian, her father, assumed his place as rightful heir to the throne of the House of Lord ThunderBane.

Of his brother Lord Popynjhay, the lightly twisted captain of the king's Royal Guard Asholthom, and the slightly malevolent wizard Haliburton, it is said they left the valley of the House of Lord ThunderBane in disgrace, departing the seacoast on a sailing vessel for landfall somewhere beyond the horizon.

And of Hahr LeQuinn and PonteFane, legend tells of a duo seen leaving the quiet valley, crossing beyond the Tranquility Mountains...

Part II

Imagine and wonder why…

Prologue

"Play was our job, our work as children. Our office was that inner world of make-believe, of curiosity, wonder, and enchantment. Years later we would find our memories and treasures kept in an old cigar box—a piece of colored twine, Grandfather's pocket watch, three marbles, the nubbin of a favorite Crayola, an Indian Head penny, a skate key. Would that we had not retired so long ago..."

~With thanks to Harper Lee for her *To Kill a Mockingbird*, and Steve Frankfurt for creation of the title sequence for the movie...

There was this place I went to as a child. It wasn't very far, and it took little effort to get there. It was a place of wonderful silences, mystery, and intrigue. It was a place in part lonely for its solitude, but mostly it gave me times rich in ways that comforted and provided sanctuary. It opened vistas otherwise unknown to a young farm boy from a working-class family in the 1950s San Joaquin Valley of California.

I worked on the family farm from a young age, often after school and sometimes after dinner, and during the triple-digit dry heat of the summer harvest. In addition to learning a strong work ethic, I experienced the cycle of seasons and our interdependent relationship to the food chain.

I worked in the spring just as the blossoms magically appeared, seeing in them a part of the cycle of birth, life and death, and rebirth.

On crisp fall days I worked to irrigate our orchards, and came to know a little of our place in the scheme of life.

Much of farm life is solitary, spent *"chasing water"* (my mom's description of irrigation) and driving the tractor, pulling a disc to turn the earth. There isn't much social about irrigating the orchards in long days of spring or driving a tractor in the wee hours of the morning—hours spent working by myself with only my thoughts for company.

During those times I found solace in this inner world, in the imagery that flooded my mind as the waters flooded our orchards, visions that turned over in my imagination as the soil was turned over in long rows behind the tractor. There was comfort there, a place warm and familiar and secure.

This is a place I still visit often, where I experience the pull of gravity lessen and am able to lift off from the earth, taking flight. Here, in my mind's eye, the mysteries of nature are opened before me in all their splendor, much as they were when first I experienced the cycles of life and death and renewal back on the farm.

Describing these experiences comes readily to me as word-images form and fill my mind. I have always loved words for their power to excite, for their ability to evoke images that give life to ideas, forming answers in the face of a child's curiosity.

In the absence of something concrete, one relies on images summoned from within to clothe words spoken by or to another. This is a uniquely human facility, and one that carries rich rewards for any who would journey to that remarkable realm within.

To a child, this is a land of make-believe, beautiful and

charming—a world wild and wonderful and enchanted. To an adult—to me—it is a place ever as real and necessary in the living of life, as vital to the nurturing of the soul as food and water are to the body.

This is a realm most of us retired from when we "grew out of childhood"—a place we sometimes return to in dreams, both night and waking, in periods of reverie, priceless and fleeting, or when we touch on that source from whence valor originates.

I consider myself one of the fortunate ones, who never really left this world behind—who carried it forward just inside my vest as I grew into adulthood. It serves as a source of comfort and strength when circumstance calls me to stretch beyond my reach, and cause for joy whenever I encounter a kindred soul who slips me the sacred handshake as a sign from within their vest.

As an adult, I still spend extended periods in this wonderland. I have always had a rich inner life, and as occasion would have it I am flooded now and again with the excitement I experienced as I witnessed the processes of creation in our orchards and vineyards. The delicate image of a flower, the sweep and grandeur of a landscape, or the flight of a granddaughter across an expanse of grass pursuing a butterfly: these transport me, their power magically loosening the hold on my mind and allowing passage to that realm where the heart dwells. They draw back the veil that dims my view and open me to the possibility of defying gravity. In revisiting the memory traces of those earlier moments, in exploring those fields today, I find I am once again chasing water.

My hope is that these short stories serve to drop a pebble into the still quiet waters of your mind, touching some aesthetic sensibility; that they open portals to that inner world of yesteryear, calling you back to the wonder-filled days of childhood, thus bringing you out of retirement...

The Wall

It stood silently in the mist, the sun lighting its expanse—a gentle northerly wind blowing, and the fog a swirling haze across its face. It loomed as an immense and forbidding presence, yet it beckoned out of the shadows of its past, and Valeri could no longer stay away. She held tightly to her grandfather's hand as they walked slowly along the promenade.

As they approached, what had been a sliver of darkness on the crest of the grassy rise began to grow. The sculpted landscape dropped away and down a slight incline, exposing an expanse of midnight-black granite, angular and powerful and calling.

The stretches of lawn were a painterly pastel green, an illusion amplified by the low-lying fog. Because of this the blackness of the granite stood in stark contrast to its soft, hazy surroundings.

Clutching harder to Grandfather's large, callused hand, she felt his warm fingers securely enfolding hers. However, despite his protective presence her steps slowed as they came near to it.

The light was diffused and soft, with shadows playing across her view. She felt warm and comfortable, even with the slight wind, and thought she could hear music ever so softly. There were voices, too—a low chatter of people talking, but there was no one else present. The voices then faded to silence, and she felt alone. *No.* Grandfather was there beside her, holding her hand.

They were standing at the western edge of the monument. As Valeri looked down the stone pathway leading along the face of the wall, she let go of Grandfather's hand.

The Washington Monument rose in the far distance, immense, a silent sentinel half hidden in the silver grey of fog surrounding everything.

Grandfather, too, stood in silence, tall and unmoving, steady, his hand ready should she need or want it. Valeri was just ten, and this trip was fully her idea. He wouldn't push his way in or intrude unless invited.

Her mother wasn't convinced she should make the trip, but Valeri was so sure.

Now, she stood at the brink, stiffened ever so slightly, and brought her shoulders up to stand taller. Under Grandfather's watchful eye, she took in a deep breath and slowly stepped forward, her eyes focused on the landing at the bottom of the sloping walkway. She was going to meet her father.

❧　　❧　　❧

Valeri's mother always said that she was quite active during the last month, kicking and turning, constantly moving. She was also late by a week, by the doctor's calculations.

Valeri was too young to remember the day she came home from the hospital. She didn't sleep much at first, and while she was awake waved her arms and kicked her feet; she was so active.

Her mother took a lot of pictures that first year, and wrote long letters to Valeri's dad, letters she would remember fondly having written much later.

The black granite wall glistened under the light touch of fog, highlighted subtly by the sun still seeking to overcome the silver grey that shrouded everything. As she walked slowly down the incline, from the corner of her eye Valeri could see the granite, black as midnight, rise on her left until its level top towered above her. The wall felt warm, even though the weather was brisk. It was warm and alive because of the names.

Valeri knew why these names were here. Grandfather, who had researched the location before they came to Washington, just that morning gave her a slip of paper with her father's name on it, along with his new home address: Panel 135-East, Line 21.

Valeri was one year old when the men in uniforms came to their front door. Grandfather and Grandmother had been visiting for the weekend; as her mother told the story years later, they helped her through the initial shock of the bad news. Valeri didn't remember this day or her mother crying, since she was so young at the time.

When she was three, Valeri had invited Melanie and Paige and Billy to her birthday party. It was a lot of fun, the first birthday she can remember. At the end, when their moms and dads came to pick them up, Valerie for the first time asked her mother, "Where is my daddy?"

She remembered how her mother struggled to answer her and cried. Valeri didn't understand, and didn't ask again.

Her father, Lt. Jason Lee Combs, had just one final mission to fly before ending his tour of duty in Vietnam. The year was 1972.

He had graduated from The Ohio State University with honors, an electrical engineering major and, even though he had a great job offer, enlisted in the Air Force during the last years of the war.

He completed his flight training with superior marks and was assigned to an elite fighter squadron flying escort for the B-52 bombing raids, which toward the end of the war were pounding the jungles of North Vietnam unmercifully.

On this mission a Russian-made surface-to-air missile came screaming up out of the darkness and slammed into the tail section of his aircraft. Spotters flying behind reported seeing his ship spiraling violently down, leaving a trail of thick black smoke.

There were no parachutes; pilot and copilot went down with their plane.

Valeri finally got up enough courage one day to ask Grandfather about her father—she thought this must have been when she was around seven.

Her mother loved her dearly, Valeri knew, but whenever the subject of her father came up was never able to say anything; she cried instead.

Grandfather would get wispy-eyed, too, but he would take Valeri out onto the swing in the backyard or walk with her down to the drug store for a soda. Sometimes they'd sit in the window box looking out over Mother's flower garden on the east side of the house.

Grandfather told her many stories about her dad—how they went fishing out at the lake when he was nine; about his playing football in school; the time he ran out of gas on a date and the two had to walk fifteen miles home in the rain; and about his courtship of her mother.

He told her of her dad's dreams, that he was a sensitive and special kind of man—and of him calling with the news that they were going to be grandparents.

⚔   ⚔   ⚔

Valeri stopped as she reached the landing at the bottom of the incline, seeing her reflection in the shiny surface staring back at herself.

She'd chosen to wear her new dress, the one she and her mother had shopped for several weeks earlier—it was light lavender with purple and light blue ribbons, had small lavender buttons up to her neck, and a hem cut just above her knees. With her hair pulled back, she looked so beautiful.

She could see that her face was a little tense, and she tried to relax—she didn't want to be sad when she met her father. Unconsciously, she reached out and grasped Grandfather's hand. He was right there, and the immediacy of his touch gave her courage to go on.

She looked at the wall markers and saw that she was almost there. She moved on, but slowly now, letting the names etched into the face of darkness beside her flow across the visual field of her mind.

Names. People, just like her dad. People with families, grandparents, daughters—just like her.

Stephen R Chambers—Geoffrey L Kimball—Terence Brooks.

Names. Valeri tried to see the faces that went with each name, and she closed her eyes as she reached out her hand and touched the wall, feeling spaces etched out of the granite that each stood for a person: "Charles T Emerson, III."

Jeremy Barstow was a slight boy in Valeri's third grade class. He was dark-haired, a little sickly and pale, and given to a mean temperament.

One day he was walking past a group of girls, Valeri being one of them, and called out, "Your father was a baby killer!" Jeremy got that look in his eyes, laughed and ran off.

Hurt and not understanding, Valeri went running into the classroom crying. Her teacher took her aside but was unable to console her.

When her mother arrived, she and the teacher sat with Valeri. She then, with a lot of pain, told Valeri about her father: that he was an airman who flew planes in a war that was now over; that while he had died on his last mission he loved Valeri very much, even though he never got to see her because he had been away.

Valeri asked, "Why did Jeremy say my father was a baby killer?"

The teacher sighed and said, "Some people didn't like the war very much, and thought that those who fought in it were bad people. That just wasn't so!"

*   *   *

The black wall seemed to go on and on—the names seemed endless. Valeri stopped and bent her head back to see the top of the wall. It reached to the sky, its uppermost edge softened by the lingering fog.

The names were all there, and while unspoken except as Valeri read them, they told the story of people. She thought of the little girls just like herself whose fathers had gone off to war and never returned, beginning to feel a deep ache inside.

Tears welled up and moistened her eyes, then rolled down her cheeks. She blinked and rubbed the tears away with her free hand. Grandfather stood beside her; she looked up and said, "I'd like to stop for a minute."

"Okay," he said, and waited.

Her shoulders shuddered briefly, and then she seemed to compose herself. She said softly, "I'm ready to go on now."

Trevor Newsome lived on the same block as Valeri for a time. His family moved into the Ferguson house after the old man died; the man's son had sold the house, moving away with his wife and children.

Trevor was a most curious sort, and troubled. He was very smart and knew it, enjoying making everyone around him feel dumb; he had a knack for doing that. He also had a mean streak a mile wide and bullied all the children in the neighborhood.

He lied if anyone ever told on him, and held grudges when they did. Valeri learned soon enough to avoid him; one day he started teasing that her father was a killer of innocent women and children. Trevor got that look in his eyes, laughed, and then ran off.

Valeri told her mother what Trevor said, and she put her arm around Valeri's shoulder and they sat and talked. She went over what made people so mean sometimes, then gradually drifted to talking about Valeri's father: "He was a kind and sensitive man. You would have loved to know him."

These were healing times, for her mother as well as herself, and Valeri would soon forget all about Trevor.

Panel 135-East. Valeri breathed in deeply and squeezed Grandfather's hand. She looked up at the shiny surface, and the names were all a blur, merging one into another. The wall, dark as midnight, shone in the subdued and hazy light, shifting into blue-black and shades of grey, then back to the deep darkness of outer space.

Valeri narrowed her eyes and took in a breath; now she felt calm and ready.

She looked up into Grandfather's weathered face, his warm brown eyes seeming to imply *It's okay*. He picked her up in his arms and held her tightly against his chest.

From her vantage point, Valeri counted down to Row 21, and then looked across the line of names: "Edward P Stewart," "Peter Carpenter," "Walter J Templeton," "Nathaniel S Levine," "Jason L Combs"...Jason Lee Combs, her father.

Valeri looked at the name and felt as though he looked back at her. She reached out and touched the name—her father. It felt warm, and she pushed harder against the granite. "Can I make a rubbing to take home?" she asked Grandfather.

Grandfather said, "Of course," and pulled a piece of paper from his back pocket. Reaching into his coat, he pulled out several crayons he'd brought just for that purpose.

Valeri turned toward the wall, gently placing the paper over her father's name. As she adjusted the paper just so, a hand reached over her shoulder while a voice said, "Here, let me help." Valeri looked toward the voice and right into the steady eyes of her mother.

"I'd like you to meet your father..."

One if by Land…

Dense fog shrouded the rough terrain, making it all but impossible to see more than a few yards ahead. Mole listened intently for a long time but heard nothing. Allied intelligence had put the enemy's top-secret defense in this sector, and indications were that there would be heavy resistance.

To be this close and hear nothing, and to see nothing, was troublesome in Mole's mind.

This heavy fog doesn't help, thought Mole to himself.

He caught Wolf's eye and motioned for him to swing right toward the river. McBeaver would be there by the makeshift bridge under the low-hanging trees on the riverbank. This was the narrowest point along a swiftly flowing river and would be the easiest spot to cross.

But Mole was worried—Owl, their fourth member, hadn't made contact since the OSS team dropped behind enemy lines two nights ago.

Owl's mission was to make a low-level reconnaissance flight over the cliffs along the beaches, specifically observing coastal fortifications, and report back to Mole.

Thus far, Owl hadn't made contact, and time was running out. The team had to make its move to sabotage the defensive network by 2100 hours tonight, or they would be too late. It was already 1900 hours, and the light was failing fast. The heavy fog was the main obstacle.

Wolf crept silently through the underbrush along a shallow gully, then down a slight embankment to the river's edge. The thick fog hid his movements from any observing eyes, but he still moved with all due caution and stayed mainly in the shadows. It was deathly still.

Wolf slipped silently under the low-hanging willow trees and waited.

Suddenly, there was a slight rippling of the waters to his left, and McBeaver's nose silently broke the surface. McBeaver blinked and smiled, showing a wide expanse of two large teeth. Wolf grinned back.

"What took you so long?" he quipped, but this was lost on McBeaver as he slid quickly under the surface again, coming up on the other side of the temporary bridge.

McBeaver's task was to get the team across the river without their being detected by the enemy. The makeshift bridge he had fashioned of fallen trees, twigs, a paste of mud and leaves, and berry vines, all found nearby, would do the trick.

Wolf was impressed, though because of the skills demanded of each team member on the mission, he wasn't surprised.

Wolf and McBeaver would wait until dark, which would be in just ninety minutes, and then make their move.

Mole would join them at the appointed hour at the water's edge.

However, without Owl's reconnaissance information they would be working in the dark, in more ways than one.

McBeaver knew the reason Owl hadn't made contact was that he was either dead or captured.

Wolf believed otherwise, for he knew Owl, and understood he was considerably more than resourceful. Although late, Wolf knew

Owl would be there at the right time, and with the necessary information. Owl would not fail the mission.

In the headquarters bunker cut deep into the cliffs overlooking the beaches, Commanding General Herr Jyai Snake was making final plans to repel the Allied invasion he knew was imminent. His intelligence sources put the Allied attack at this location, and the commanding position of the defensive bunkers gave a sweeping view of the beaches along the coast.

He was calm and deliberate as he spoke quietly with his second and third in command, Vice Commandant Tohmas Leopard of the Fourth Lightning Panther Division and General Gymm Coyote, known among Allied commanders as the stealthy Desert Fox.

Commanding General Snake believed the extensive array of bunkers carved into the solid rock cliffs overlooking the beaches, alongside the mystical powers of the AirHead race, would prove invincible to the combined powers of the Allied forces. It would be like shooting fish in a barrel.

Vice Commandant Leopard paced back and forth, being nervous by nature. By character and reputation he was a fierce combatant, cunning and terribly ruthless. Those who served under him feared his wrath as much as his foes did. General Coyote, for his part, had a mean streak the width of his ego, which was vast indeed.

In a firefight, Coyote was vicious and unrelenting, and gave no quarter. He moved his troops with amazing speed and had defeated the best the Allied commanders in Northern Africa could throw against him. His command of military strategy, both theoretical as well as time-tested and practical, was considerable. There were few his equal.

Commanding General Snake had indeed gathered together his top military minds for the defense of the Third Right.

⹂   ⹂   ⹂

Mole was deeply concerned as he met the others at the river's edge. It was time to move, and there was still no word from Owl. The crossing had to be made, but without Owl's information, how would they know where to scale the cliffs? And how would they know which bunkers at the top were real, and which decoys? Mole didn't like this at all.

"Damn," he muttered half aloud. Wolf appeared suddenly out of the darkness beside him, and Mole jumped, though he caught himself before he let out a scream.

"Don't do that!" whispered Mole testily.

"Sorry," said Wolf, smiling broadly. "And stop worrying. Owl will be here."

Mole looked into the steady eyes of Wolf and shook his head. "I'm afraid we haven't the time to find out; we have to go without him," said Mole, "and do the best we can."

"Begging your pardon, Captain," said Wolf, holding Mole's eyes. "Owl wouldn't let the team down; he'll be here."

Just then, McBeaver surfaced silently at the water's edge.

"The bridge is ready," McBeaver said matter-of-factly to Mole. He had attached the floating bridge to the banks on both sides of the river and covered the logs and vines with a thin layering of moss and algae, giving it a wet and watery look that was difficult to see in the dark.

Mole was impressed; Wolf, again, was not surprised.

The three mounted the bridge and crossed quickly and easily, unseen in the darkness. As they reached the opposite bank and headed for the tree cover, there was a rush of wind and the stroke of powerful wings, and Owl swooped down to join his comrades.

Wolf smiled and winked as Mole caught his eye. Mole smiled in return. He then asked Owl to report on things since their drop behind enemy lines.

Owl said his liftoff had been delayed because of the heavy fog, and he couldn't radio in without alerting the enemy of his presence. So he'd taken a chance that the team would either proceed without him and make the best of the mission or that he'd get to the rendezvous point on time with his information.

As it turned out, the fog had lifted near the crest of the cliffs, so he was able to fly reconnaissance and photograph the fortifications anyway.

"I have the information you need," said Owl. Wolf smiled.

"Hmmm," said Mole.

Owl laid out photographs of the cliff area and quickly identified the cruel paths that led up the towering cliffs, noting which of the bunkers were sham and which real.

Mole, Wolf, and McBeaver listened intently. When Owl concluded his report, Mole nodded his head and said, "It's time. You all know what you have to do."

As Owl and McBeaver took their places in the shadows nearby, Mole and Wolf smudged their faces with the soot from burnt cork, and each checked their sidearm—government issue Colt 45 semi-automatic pistols.

When they were ready, without a word Mole and Wolf slipped into the darkness alongside the sheer cliffs. It was still pitch dark as they began their ascent.

At first the way was steep but easily negotiated by the two. Soon the pathways narrowed and disappeared; climbing now requiring more and more use of paws and nails to grasp holds amidst the cracks and crevices. Both Mole and Wolf were in excellent condition, and while the climb was difficult, they moved quickly up the face of the cliff.

Mole and Wolf reached an area on the cliffs just below the crest where all the defensive bunkers were. They had made it in the extreme darkness without alerting any of the elite troops guarding the bunkers.

Carefully, though with speed and urgency, they placed time-delayed explosives just beneath the gunports of each of the actual bunkers.

They set the timers to coincide with the massive invasion to come, with the hope the explosions would cause havoc amidst the elite troops of Commanding General Jyai Snake, lessening their advantage.

McBeaver, who had remained below to guard the floating bridge, covered the retreat of Mole and Wolf with his Browning automatic rifle poised.

Owl was lookout, and in the darkness eluded enemy radar by flying just inches off the sheer face of the cliffs. He provided additional support and coverage for Mole and Wolf with his Thompson submachine gun.

※　　※　　※

Just as Wolf reached the lower section of the narrow pathway, a shot rang out of the looming darkness. A shock of pain ripped through his shoulder into his chest, and Wolf slumped to his knees, tumbling down the remainder of the pathway.

Mole was the first to reach Wolf, followed by Owl. Wolf wasn't moving, and Owl let out a low moan, rolling his eyes.

McBeaver came up and watched as Mole applied pressure to the bleeding wound in Wolf's chest. He told Mole he would return shortly, then slipped into the shadows and was gone.

Wolf lay lifeless on the sandy ground at the foot of the cliff as Mole worked over him.

Finally, Owl said, "He's gone, Mole; you gotta stop. It's getting light, and enemy snipers will be looking for us. We gotta get outta here."

Mole sat back and let out a long, low sigh. "You're right, Owl. He's gone. But we can't leave him here."

Just then, McBeaver returned. "Come on," he whispered, "I have the bridge ready. We just have time to make it." And with that the three carried their fallen comrade the short distance to the river's edge.

McBeaver had severed the vines holding the bridge onto the opposite bank and cut away portions of the bridge so less than an eighth of it remained attached to the banks on this side. The three got on board, carrying the lifeless body of Wolf, and gently set him down in the center of the makeshift raft.

McBeaver cut through the remaining vines holding the bridge in place, and it floated free. With powerful flips of his tail, McBeaver guided the raft into the main current of the river, and they floated swiftly downstream. In minutes the river carried the four past the beaches and out into dark ocean waters.

As the morning light broke, a lone PT boat made a sweep across the ocean off the beaches of Normandy and picked up three weary soldiers clinging to a small raft, along with their dead comrade and companion.

During this maneuver, Commanding General Jyai Snake's elite

troops laid down an intense barrage of artillery fire directed at the lone rescue boat.

In moments one of the time-delayed explosives malfunctioned, blowing up a day premature and wiping out the central command bunker.

Three top military strategists of the enemy's command were killed, and a major segment of the defensive deployment was destroyed, causing havoc amidst the preparations for the defense of the Third Right.

Two if by Sea...

Sandi listened to the waves lap the shore as she walked down the beach, the morning sun to her back. Last night had been a little cooler, the harbinger of the coming fall, but it was still warm enough now that she wore only a light T-shirt and shorts. She felt the coolness of the sand between her toes, a light breeze playing in her hair.

It had been a long quiet summer with no one to bother her. No media to shout obscene headlines at her, no telephones breaking the pure silences, and only her dad and Terrapin to keep her company.

Terrapin was her constant companion, her confidante, the best four-footed therapist and friend in all the world. The feelings were mutual.

Terrapin had raced ahead, romping along the beach, barking and leaping at several gulls basking in sunlight along the water's edge. With little effort they lifted into the air and gently landed thirty yards down the beach, well out of harm's way.

Then, in a flurry of wet fur and happy senseless yapping, Terrapin raced back to Sandi and screeched to a halt at her feet.

He nudged her leg as she approached a dip in the sand, and she instinctively slowed her pace in synch with Terrapin's lead.

Then, above the sound of the waves, she heard her name being shouted. It was harsh, a shock, and brought her suddenly back from another world. Her dad was calling for her to have breakfast.

"Come on, Terp," said Sandi, and she trotted off in the direction of the beach house as Terp padded along beside her.

᠌ᡰ   ᡰ   ᡰ

The smell of bacon and a spicy omelet and toast greeted Sandi as she slid the glass door open and entered from the deck. Terrapin followed her in, and she left the door ajar to let the breeze blow through.

Sandi held her father's face and kissed him on the cheek. "Hi, Dad," she said, then sat across the table from him. "Thanks for not pushing," she added.

"Hey, my time's your time," he replied through a smile. "So how was the sunrise?"

Sandi looked in his direction and smiled. "I didn't notice, Dad...I guess my mind was somewhere else."

"Couldn't sleep last night?" he asked.

"No, not much," she replied. "I took a walk down the beach a little after midnight. The weather reports said the moon was out, and it was quiet—did you know the sound of the waves is like white noise from beyond our galaxy?"

Dad smiled, his blue eyes sparkling. Sandi pushed the eggs around on her plate, obviously preoccupied and troubled. Dad silently ate his eggs and munched on a piece of burnt toast with strawberry jam dripping off the edges.

Sandi cleared her throat, and Dad paused, not saying anything. "Dad," whispered Sandi.

"Yes," replied Dad, his voice firm and steady, also just a whisper.

"I have a problem, and I don't know what to do about it," she continued.

"Umhmm," said Dad.

"There's a situation at the lab—one involving several people that are important to my project, but who are acting like total jerks." Her voice rose a little but remained under control, still little more than a whisper.

Dad nodded his head, lips set and eyes locked with hers.

Sandi's eyes always took his breath away, they were so much like her mother's—hazel, bordering on green, and deep as a glacier-fed lake. And there was always a fire burning somewhere deep down.

When she smiled, it was like a crisp morning—and for Dad it awakened an ache deep inside. He loved Sandi's mother very much, and still hadn't gotten over her sudden death from cancer five years ago.

It was she who encouraged Sandi to pursue astral physics despite her blindness, and it was she who was Sandi's greatest strength from undergrad through to graduation from Harvard, summa cum laude.

"Dad, I've been director of Project Orbit Saturn since its inception. Now, Tobar Narquist, coordinator of projects at the National Union of Transient-Technology, is blocking my project because of some insane paranoia that the Japanese are stealing our data. Of course the Japanese are collaborating with our project, and are underwriting joint research into transient-technological phenomenon. Narquist knows about the collaboration but refuses to acknowledge their efforts."

Dad listened, clucked his tongue, and put his hand on Sandi's forearm.

"He and Julius Burwell—he's our controller—sent me an audio memo yesterday, saying that Project Orbit Saturn is temporarily on hold, at least until the Senate Finance Subcommittee has a chance to review our last two years' data."

Sandi sighed and muttered under her breath, "Shit...!"

Dad smiled and squeezed her forearm. Then he reached over, lifted her chin until her eyes were level with his, and said, "Sandi, you're a fighter. This is merely one roadblock, and you must know your project has the highest levels of support. Your colleagues across the country know you're on the right track—and they support you, even the men. Just hang in there."

Dad paused a moment, then continued, "You know that jerks like Nelton and Burson will always do their best to subvert your work for what they consider the better good, but whatever their best efforts, they can't hold a candle to you and your stubborn will. I know you, honey."

"I appreciate that, Dad, but you haven't heard the latest. Jules Guildor was appointed director of the National Astral-Space Technology Institute...! He has the president's ear, and Jules is as paranoid as Nelton and Burson."

Dad chuckled and took Sandi by the hand. "Let's take a walk down the beach, honey."

≿　　≿　　≿

Sandi slipped through the sliding glass door, followed by her father. They stepped off the deck onto the pathway through the ice plant. Sandi walked ahead.

"Dad, I said I didn't know what to do." She paused in thought as they strolled along the beach. "If I take a stand on principle, I may make points in the short run, and I know I'll feel one hellova lot better—but these are small men with small minds and enormous egos. They aren't above taking it out on my project out of sheer spite. The project could be lost!"

The crunching of the sand under their feet punctuated the lapping of the waves.

"But if I do nothing, they could hold the project hostage at their whims, and it would abort before having a chance. I lose either way—the project loses either way…!"

Dad could hear a fire building in Sandi's voice. She still spoke just above a whisper, and Dad had to concentrate to hear her over the lapping of the waves at their feet, but he was glad—the inner fires were being stoked, and that old glint in Sandi's eyes had returned.

"As I recall, honey, those are the very challenging odds you've cherished your whole life!" said Dad with a chuckle.

Sandi stopped and turned toward her father, grabbing his arm and punching him playfully on the shoulder. "Stop laughing at me, Dad," she shouted, also chuckling.

Terrapin, who had been padding silently alongside Sandi, barked sharply. He ran down the beach barking, then ran back and jumped up on her, getting his wet paws all over her T-shirt.

He barked again. Sandi hollered back, and grabbing Terrapin they tumbled down onto the sandy beach in a tangle of arms and legs.

Dad sat down on the sand and watched and smiled. Sandi lay back on the beach, Terrapin resting his head on her chest.

"Dad, how can I have support at the highest levels if the president is in these jerks' pockets?" asked Sandi.

Dad didn't answer at first.

Sandi turned onto her side, and propping her hand under her ear asked, "Dad…?"

"I suppose I was thinking of the president's wife, honey," he said, his eyes fixed on the morning sun highlighting her dark hair. "She's come out in support of you, and she's been very vocal about the importance of this project continuing. She's gathered others—the director of the Science Foundation, for one. Then there's Dr. Falcone, head of the Science Underwriters and director of the Department of Energy. It's only a matter of time, and the president will be yours, too," said Dad. "He hasn't a chance in the long run."

Sandi turned in her father's direction, a puzzled look on her face. "Where did you get all this?" she asked.

Dad laughed again. "Listen—your mother was privy to a number of those inner circles that most people don't even know exist. Hell, I never knew until they contacted me one day. And, because of the esteem they held for your mother, they've kept in touch with me over the years."

Dad paused. "They are the stuff of black budgets, secret agencies, and conspiracy theories, and who knows what else. Anyway, let's just say I have it on good authority that you are being watched—they're very interested in your work with transient-technology, and they won't let it fail. It's bigger than you and these little men with littler minds."

≥   ≥   ≥

The next day, Sandi received a second memorandum from Nelton and Burson. The message indicated that the Senate Finance Subcommittee was subpoenaing her to answer questions related to the project. The tone of the memo was not a good one—it gave her a sense of darkness and foreboding.

Sandi shuddered upon hearing the message. She wasn't worried about answering questions regarding the project—that she could handle in her sleep. It was the shadowy motives and hidden agenda of the committee members she was uneasy about.

She handed the message to her dad, who listened to it and smiled broadly.

"You're going to be fine, honey," he said. "They're not going to know what to do with you, trust me."

Sandi wasn't so sure.

⌇　　⌇　　⌇

On Monday, October 5th, Dr. Sandra Jeanne Pendleton, Ph.D., director of Project Orbit Saturn, appeared before the Senate Finance Subcommittee to answer questions put forth by esteemed members of the committee.

After two hours of intense and difficult probing questioning, which Dr. Pendleton managed with exceptional clarity, directness, and precision, the subcommittee took a recess.

⌇　　⌇　　⌇

The chair, Laurel Kauffman, D-Colorado, came over to Sandi and sat down on the corner of her table.

"You're doing extremely well, Dr. Pendleton," she said with not a little praise.

"Thank you, Senator," replied Sandi, smiling.

"You know why you're here, don't you? Why we've summoned you?" asked Senator Kauffman, her eyes alight.

Sandi hesitated, noting the tenor of her voice, then replied, "I don't think I understand."

"Come, come, Dr. Pendleton," chided Senator Kauffman with mock irritation. "You are obviously where you are because you're not only intelligent, with a convincing command of language to describe your research, but you also have contacts in places people shouldn't have. You are *very* well connected, Dr. Pendleton."

Senator Kauffman paused to let her comment sink in. "There are people who want your work to continue, Dr. Pendleton, people who wield power to see that it does—unbelievable power. I have followed your career for some time, and have supported you and your project from the beginning, but I have deep concerns about how you are garnering support for your work. I have fears for our country, fears for who you are lying down with…"

Senator Kauffman's voice trailed off. She leaned down to touch Sandi's arm and whispered, "Be careful, my dear—be very careful…"

She slid off the table, turned and walked to the dais, taking her seat.

✈   ✈   ✈

After a twenty-minute recess the subcommittee members returned to their seats, and the hearing resumed.

Senator Burgess Anderson, D-New York, asked for the floor, and addressing Chairperson Kauffman moved that the subcommittee recommend approval of the Project Orbit Saturn budget for the full term of the project. The silence was palpable.

Dr. Pendleton's eyes widened, though she couldn't see the faces of the subcommittee members.

"Second," said Senator Kari Stevens, R-Alaska.

"Move the question," said Senator William Hobbs, R-Arizona.

Senator Kauffman looked to the Sergeant at Arms, who began the roll-call vote:

"Senator Anderson?"

"Aye."

"Senator Benton?"

"Aye."

"Senator Garry?"

"Aye."

"Senator Hobbs?"

"Aye."

"Senator Stevens?"

"Aye."

"Senator Waverly?"

"Aye."

"Chairperson Kauffman?"

"Aye."

Senator Kauffman looked up and down the bench, and then at Sandi. Smiling, she said, "Dr. Pendleton, as you've heard, you have pleased the subcommittee, and your wish is our command—at least for the moment."

Dr. Pendleton stood and thanked each subcommittee member in turn. "I appreciate your trust, Senator Kauffman—you and the subcommittee members. I shall remember your caveat."

Sandi's Dad met her at the airport. She told him the subcommittee's decision, and he chuckled and said, "See? Nothing to worry about!"

"Right, Dad—now, let's talk about those inner circles that most people don't even know exist…"

Tiptoe Through the Mind Field

The old grandfather clock in the hall chimed the half-hour.

Owl looked up from his book and over his reading glasses at the hands of the clock; it was 12:30 in the morning. They were late.

He turned his head toward the picture window overlooking the western meadow, where lights and shadows played under a full moon. Owl looked at the clock and blinked one eye.

He swung around at the sound of a knock at the door—urgent, yet quiet.

Owl padded to the front door and opened it. Standing there in the circle of his front porch light were Sparrow and Mole.

"Come in, come in," said Owl.

The two entered and Owl took their coats. He motioned them in the direction of the sitting room.

Owl followed them into the room, and the two sat next to the fireplace. Owl remained standing and put his wing on the mantle. He smiled and said, "Now, children, tell me what is so urgent that we have to meet at this hour."

Earlier that day, Owl was sitting in his courtroom at the House of Burgess when Mole entered and asked if he had time to talk about something important.

"Of course," Owl said. "Come sit down. I'm just concluding some business; I won't be long."

Mole thanked the judge but said he and Sparrow wanted to speak in private.

"May we come by your oak tree tonight around midnight?" asked Mole.

"Hmmm, that is a bit unusual, but if you think it's important, why not? I tend to be awake at that hour anyway!"

Mole thanked the judge, turned and left.

⇀   ⇀   ⇀

Mole cleared his throat and looked at Owl standing near the fireplace.

"You know that my parents are from the Woodlands to the south," said Mole.

"They came in the late '30s, as I recall, from near the Painted Desert, wasn't it?"

"Yes," Mole said, nodding. "And you know that Sparrow's parents have lived long in the Evergreen Forest."

Owl nodded back and smiled.

"You've known the two of us since we were children, Judge Owl," said Mole. "We played together down by the river during the summers, and bundled up in woolens when the snows came. We even went to the same school near the Painted Desert. When Sparrow left to attend flight college and I stayed and entered the mining engineering program at Evergreen University, we kept in touch through pigeon-mail."

"Yes, I recall Sparrow's parents telling me so," said Owl. "And when you both graduated with honors from your respective universities, your parents were so proud."

"Yes," said Mole. Mole looked at Sparrow and the two looked back at Owl.

"You're telling me that you are what your generation calls 'an item?'" asked Owl.

Mole looked surprised, while Sparrow, embarrassed, smiled and nodded.

"How did you..." stammered Mole.

"How did I know?" interrupted Owl. "Come, come. You are both so obviously in love I would have to be sleep-flying to miss it." He smiled, big eyes gleaming. "So, what is the problem then, children? Why the secrecy?"

Sparrow sighed. "It was so easy when we were young. No one said anything when we played together, or when we had classes together."

"All of a sudden being different became an issue—and some began to whisper behind our backs when they heard that we were exchanging pigeon-mails," said Mole. "Then, during holiday break, it was all raised eyebrows and clucking tongues when they saw us together at Finch's Fountain."

Owl nodded and came to sit down across the coffee table from his young guests. "Ahh," said Owl, "the transiency of friendship. Do any of your friends understand?"

Smiles came over their faces as they nodded.

"Hummingbird and Tortoise have stood by us, and Finch and Beaver are happy for us," said Mole. "But others have avoided us since we've returned home, and that hurts."

Sparrow had a tear in her eyes, and Owl rose and brought her a box of tissues.

"What about your parents?" asked Owl. "Where are they in all this?"

Owl listened as Sparrow shared that her parents were stunned at first and had wanted her to marry a nice bird of a feather from the Evergreen Forest. "They are taking it very hard. They know Mole and like him as a friend," she said, "but the idea of us getting married—well, they're..."

Mole sighed. "My parents are having a difficult time. They wouldn't even talk with me about it for a long while. God knows I tried—but they're pretty upset. This has never happened in our family before, ever, and they're more concerned with what creatures in the Woodlands and Dunes will say. I don't know what they'll do if we go ahead with the wedding."

Sparrow nodded and said, "Mine, too."

⇗　　⇗　　⇗

Owl got up and went over to the large picture window. He was deep in thought, but his demeanor remained light and upbeat.

Mole cleared his throat, and the sound brought Owl back.

"Well, children," said Owl, "I think the time has come to take some forthright steps!" Turning to them, he took a small slip of paper from under his wing and held it out to Sparrow.

"Here, this will gain you audience with a friend of mine who is versed in these matters. I have mentioned this to him, and he awaits your call."

Mole looked at Sparrow, and both turned puzzled expressions to Owl.

"Hmm, yes, um," said Owl, "I took the liberty of discussing your plight with my friend several days ago, and he said of course he would meet with you. How did I come to already discuss this with someone when I just heard from you tonight?" Owl posed rhetorically to himself.

"Well, I have known both your parents for a long time, even before you both were born. I know you two very well. And, I am somewhat skilled in reading people and their unsaid thoughts. Your parents are neither bad people nor unreadable, frankly."

Owl sat down next to Sparrow and handed her the business card.

"Who is this friend?" asked Mole. "And how can he help us?"

Owl chuckled and touched Mole on his knee. "He's a social worker, and he's very good at what he does. His name is Harlequin Duck, and you can reach him through his email address there on his card."

Mole held the card up to the light: FlyByKnight@flock.com.

"Here, you can use the computer in my office," Owl said. He led the young couple into the next room.

Mole typed in Owl's password, typed a message, and hit the send key.

"It's gone," he said to Sparrow. "I hope it works."

⸱ ⸱ ⸱

"We've got email!" shouted Mole, his eyes aglow.

Owl joined the young lovebirds at the monitor and read the message on the screen:

"Hi y'all, meaning Sparrow & Mole," it began. "I have time 3:00 tomorrow—can we meet at my office in the Forest Mall? We'll go for a soda at Finch's Fountain."

Mole clicked the reply button. He typed in, "3:00 is fine. We'll be there," and was ready to send.

"Ask him if we need to bring anything," whispered Sparrow.

Mole typed in a p.s. and hit the reply button.

Owl put his wings around Mole's and Sparrow's shoulders. "You're going to like Harley," he said, "and not to worry. Things are going to happen now."

⸱ ⸱ ⸱

149

Harlequin Duck was an outgoing friendly bird, a free spirit who had an easy way with words and a twinkle in his light brown eyes that lit up his face.

He always wore a tie, but it was never tied tight, and the color didn't quite go with his shirt. His shirt was rumpled, and his sleeves were rolled up partway. His shoes were scuffed, and the sole of the left had a hole in it, showing his sock when he crossed his legs. His crown feathers were ruffled.

Sparrow liked him immediately, and he hadn't said or done anything yet.

Mole looked Harlequin up and down, then did a double take.

"Do you like chocolate truffles?" asked Harlequin, catching the couple off guard.

"Umhmm," the two said, nodding shyly.

"Here, there's this nice little shop around the corner that caters to one's worst and most devilish delights," he said, and chuckled.

⌇　　⌇　　⌇

"So, how do you know Judge Owl?" asked Harlequin as they sat down and ordered their chocolate treats.

"Umm, our parents have been friends for a long time, and he's known us since we were born," started Sparrow.

"Yeah, he's known us all our lives," said Mole.

Harlequin smiled. "Owl and I go way back, too. We were in undergraduate school together at the Mockingbird Institute of Evergreen Forest, and he went on to law school while I went to graduate school for social work. Those were the days!"

"Now, I want you both to relax. We can take what time we need, and we'll get to your concerns soon enough. But first tell me about yourselves," said Harlequin. He sat back to listen.

For the next forty-five minutes the two spoke about their child-hoods. Harlequin nodded often, his smile easing their discomfort at talking to someone largely a stranger. Harlequin's manner soothed their tensions, and they relaxed into a comfortable rhythm of sharing anecdotes, laughing about certain events while their eyes teared up over others.

In the end, Harlequin heard enough to give him a sense of the two lovebirds and what they were leading up to with their concerns.

"Okay, tell me, what are your parents like?" asked Harlequin.

"My dad's very strict," said Mole, "and not very flexible."

"Umhmm."

"He's a civil engineer specializing in tunnels, and very good at his job."

"What kind of music does he like?" asked Harlequin.

"Umm, mostly classical," answered Mole, "but he also likes Willie Nuthatch and Reba Nightingale."

"Hmmm," said Harlequin, "a man after my own heart! What about your mother? What does she do, and what's her music?"

"Well, she's an archaeologist at the university, and is more into religious music—you know, church-type music."

"What about your folks, Sparrow?"

"My mom's into light rock and jazz, and my dad likes the golden oldies from the '50s. I kinda like them myself."

"And what do they do?" asked Harlequin.

"My mom used to be a flight attendant, but when I came along she took to technical writing and works at home electronically. It was nice having her around while I was growing up. And my dad is chief air traffic controller at the international airport."

⸱⸱⸱

Mole sat forward and asked, "Why do you want to know all this about our parents?" There was a tinge of impatience in his voice.

"Oh, just so's I'd know a little more about you two," Harlequin answered. "You know, you're an awful lot like them...!"

Mole sat back as though he'd been struck, and Sparrow put her wingtip to her beak, a frown wrinkling her brow.

"Hey, relax...! You'd think I'd just said you had the biggest zits on your noses! Of course you're like them, how could you not be?" Putting down a generous bill to cover their treats, Harlequin stood and motioned for the two to come with him.

As they walked Harlequin listened, and his eyes glowed with an energy that touched Sparrow and Mole.

They shared more about their parents, and some about each other. Harlequin said things like:

"You're not so very different..."

and "How could they do anything other...?"

and "Your dreams aren't too far off from theirs..."

By the time they reached the edge of the Meadowlands, Sparrow shook her head. "I feel things aren't as confused as I had thought. I didn't realize how difficult this has been for my parents. You know, it occurs to me they've not forbidden us from getting married. Deep inside they want what's best for us." A gleam came back into Sparrow's eyes, and she cried a little. "They're having a tough time because we're doing something really different from anything they've ever done, and change is hard."

Mole nodded and put his arm around Sparrow's shoulders.

"Hey, you've just made a very good start," said Harlequin, and he winked and grasped both their hands. "Maybe that's enough for today, but how about we get another chocolate truffle just for good measure...?"

Dream Catcher

The sun rose into an azure sky, seemingly intent on scorching what remained of moisture from the broad plateau. Storm clouds were gathering to the west, but while some atmospheric madness was causing spectacular lightning storms there, the storm made no movement in this direction.

Truman Singleton sat next to the low mud wall in the shadow of a rock outcrop, a stand of willow trees also providing shade. He fanned himself, but even this little effort was draining, and sweat rolled down his back like the river that centuries ago ran through the ancient plateau.

The air hung heavy and oppressive over the entire region, the high humidity aggravated by the rising heat. Dr. Singleton was out of the sun, though with little benefit, and wished it would rain and get it all over with; this stifling weather was wreaking havoc with his dig team.

Dr. Singleton was one of those seekers of antiquity not only with a knack for finding fascinating locations with remarkable timelines reaching into the distant past, but who you also sensed had lived in those times. He seemed to know things about a people who lived in a region, or a cliff dwelling, that one couldn't know from just what was pulled from the earth and dusted off.

Most who met him initially found him eccentric, strange even, though with an incredible sense of humor—he did make one laugh.

His peers believed him pretentious and given to an interpretive style that in their view relied more on science fiction than scientific method.

His approach to antiquity suggested either he was a buffoon and a jester who took things lightly, or someone with incredible insight into things and places not accessible to the normal bent of even his colleagues.

Those who held to the former view discounted him and discredited his work; the latter watched his progress with rapt fascination and applause.

All of this did little good for his reputation, particularly with his colleagues, though he was oblivious of much of this, and what he was aware of he dismissed as unimportant in the larger scheme of things. In the end, this was what drew students to him and his research teams, and that was what was important.

⅋   ⅋   ⅋

Dr. Carrie Fishburn was Dr. Singleton's colleague of seventeen years, another old soul with inexplicable connections to the earth and its peoples, especially of the ancient and long-deceased type. She was a brilliant archaeologist and a classic scholar, though little recognized for her seven-volume treatise *Dwellers of the Cerro Madre*, a little-known people thought to be descendants of the Pueblo.

She was shy and of essence an introvert, an endearing quality in Dr. Singleton's mind, and what drew him to her. She thought it not so much an endearing quality, but simply a sexist projection for which she rode Dr. Singleton unmercifully. Shyness can be a convenient ploy of the intelligent that keeps the unimaginative at bay, providing the means to avoid certain encounters at will.

Students of vision, however, those with unfettered intellects and who loved the earth and its peoples (mostly of the ancient and long-deceased type) were drawn to her, and she to them. Being with her was the point. This was how it was with Dr. Singleton as well.

⸙　⸙　⸙

The low wall had been discovered the day before by one of the students working in Dr. Fishburn's section. It was the first substantial evidence of a possible site connected with Coronado's journeys into the southwestern United States during the mid-1500s.

While a far cry from Cibola and the Cities of Gold, this mud wall was a major find, and the students of the team were still reeling with the significance of it.

Dr. Singleton and Dr. Fishburn were excited, too, and had risen with the dawn, filled with anticipation over beginning their careful and closer examination of the mud wall. Several of the students were up as well, and there was anticipation in the air.

⸙　⸙　⸙

The storm clouds gathering in regions to the west on the previous day, however, had shifted, and massive and dark thunderheads had moved in and now blanketed the mesa. The anticipation was more than palpable.

Periodic lightning strikes lit up the skies and the vast arid plateau, the harbinger, Dr. Fishburn knew, of the deluge to come. She knew there would be precious little to accomplish once the rains began, so directed team members to batten everything down, clear the common tent areas, and settle down with a good book.

The eager students worked quickly. Although there was a bit of disappointment at the postponement of scrutinizing the ancient wall, they relished the idea of spending "down time" with Dr. Fishburn, hearing stories and anecdotes from her previous digs.

Long jagged flashes seared the darkening skies, throwing everything momentarily into the brightness of a hundred suns before abruptly falling back into shadows.

Lightning strikes crashed into the mesa close by, making the surrounding air electric and giving off that distinctive odor of ozone. Almost immediately the skies seemed to unbuckle, and thunder engulfed everyone in a bone-shaking grasp, felt mainly from the top of the forehead to a point just behind the eyes. The heavens opened, and the rains came.

❧　❧　❧

Everyone was gathered in the main tent when Dr. Singleton threw back the large tent flap and entered. Someone kidded him about the increase in his intelligence, since he came in out of the rain. The group laughed, as did he.

The lights flickered with the crash of nearby thunder, and then went out, everything sinking into pitch blackness.

Someone cursed, and another said, "There goes the main generator!"

Dr. Singleton was conscious of the stillness as he struck a light. The match flared, sending plumes of sulfur into the air and illuminating the space around him.

❧　❧　❧

For a moment he became disoriented, for none of the others were around, and he was no longer in the main tent.

He found himself staring into a deeply tanned face, wrinkled and creased with the folds of wisdom and framed in long, silver white hair pulled back behind the ears.

Her eyes were deep pools, blue-grey and passionate. They caught the glint of the match's flame—smiling, she took his hand and led him out of the cave's entrance, onto the wide mesa.

"Who are you?" he asked, his voice just a whisper. "And where are we?"

The woman said not a word but raised her arm and pointed in the direction of the eastern horizon, where the dark of midnight was giving way to the lavenders and amber of morning.

Wispy clouds caressed the mountain ridge, making faint formations in the growing light. In slow motion they grew to huge thunderheads, and lightning flashed, the low rumble of thunder echoing across the valley in between.

Then the clouds grew fainter and the lightning ceased, but the thunder remained, although only as a hint of its former boldness.

❧   ❧   ❧

The clouds moved in a slow dance across the low eastern sky, swirling into a ceremonial shield, the center of which was a circular form with delicate interlacing webbing across the middle, two eagle feathers hanging down from either side—a dream catcher.

As Dr. Singleton watched, the clouds shifted and moved yet again, now leaving faint images just above the distant ridges: the images of three men. "These were gods who came to this mesa and into the valley below many years ago," said the woman softly. "They rode on magnificent creatures—creatures that breathed fire, peals of thunder coming from their hooves."

The woman's eyes flashed with wonderment, tinged with the hint of anger. "They came with followers of the same spirit. Their skin was light as the clouds in the sky, their eyes the hue of a mountain lake—and they carried sticks that brought thunder out of the skies, and many of the people fell before them."

The woman's blue-grey eyes burned with a passion, but she spoke barely above a whisper.

"Then they did the unspeakable: they raped and murdered the daughter of the chief of the Cerro Madre. And they walked freely among the people, who were sore afraid."

Dr. Singleton noted a deep sadness in the woman's eyes. She paused.

"But the medicine spirits of the mesa were very powerful, and brought a curse upon the three gods, and banished them to the lands beyond the Valley of Creation. The powerful medicine spirits gave them names, so the people would know them should their paths ever cross—Travels over Mesa, Journeys into Mountains, and Jumps above Yellowsun.

"Travels over Mesa was the meanest, and was transformed into the Gila monster, cursed to roam the hot desert sands on his belly for the rest of his days.

"Journeys into Mountains, a master of deceit and cruelty, was changed into the deadly scorpion, banished to live under rocks and in dark places, and hated by man for all eternity.

"Jumps above Yellowsun spoke with a forked tongue, and true to his nature became the sidewinder serpent. He, too, was cursed to live in the barren desert and hated by man."

The woman held Dr. Singleton's gaze. "The medicine spirits were too great for the others, and they, too, left the mesa and the valleys below, and with their magnificent creatures traveled to the northeast.

"My people then left the mesa and traveled to the south. They live there still," she whispered, her eyes glistening. Dr. Singleton reached out and touched his fingers to the woman's cheek, wiping away a tear.

There was suddenly a flare of intense light, and Dr. Singleton shielded his eyes against its brilliance. When he opened them, he held a lit match in his hand, its glow spreading in a circle around him, illuminating the space in the large tent.

He could see several people seated on canvas-backed chairs and on cases on the ground.

"Thanks for the match, Dr. Singleton," said a voice out of the darkness. "If you'd light the lantern, I'll get to work on the generator..."

The Battle of Byte Mountain

Lance Corporal Presseny Key sat huddled under his rain slicker and peered through the gathering darkness across the deadly expanse of no-man's land. Heavy storms had obscured the mountain for most of the day, drenching everything in a downpour of the magnitude of Noah's plight.

Now, aside from the steady pounding of the heavy rains, an eerie silence hung over the battlefield, casting an even darker pall over the surrounding woods and fields.

It was the worst of days, and for Lance Corporal Key, time stood still. He knew, though, that Lt. Ramis Beauregard, Ram Beau to the troops, would soon be giving the order to advance up the mountain—then, time would run backwards.

Lance Corporal Key was numb with fear, wanted to run in the opposite direction and hide from all this horror.

He pulled his rain slicker tighter around his shoulders and upper torso, trying to keep his powder horn under the protection of his now-soaked overcoat. It was a losing battle—just like the fight for bragging rights to the top of the mountain. That's what it seemed like the coming battle was all about, though his superiors said it was probably more than that.

Probably!

Lance Corporal Key's regiment had laid siege to the lower flanks of this devil mountain for the better part of a week. Their losses were heavy, and for all that sacrifice they had made pitifully little progress in capturing the mountaintop. Many of his regiment were casualties in a battle that neither he nor they understood, one which seemed surely destined for failure.

He had himself sustained a superficial wound on his upper leg in an early morning assault two days ago. Over nine thousand casualties were sustained that day alone, in a combined total for both sides.

While his injury wasn't painful or in any way incapacitating, he knew in time it could mean the loss of his leg, or worse, the drawing of his last breath. That prospect loomed in the back of his mind, all the more because of the penetrating cold.

The battle for Byte Mountain proper began twenty days ago, and both sides were paying an extremely high toll. Lt. Ram Beau was thrust into command of the 34th Massachusetts Regiment on the first day of battle after Capt. N. Sufficient Memory was cut down by a withering fusillade from above.

The Confederates were well-entrenched on the upper ridges, and might just as well have thrown rocks down upon the Union soldiers with equal effect. It would have helped the Confederates save their limited and diminishing supplies of gunpowder.

Lance Corporal Key was only able to get several shots off against Confederate sharpshooters before being pinned down himself. Others around him had the same fate, though some were much worse off for their efforts and would not see the light of the next day.

Lt. Ram Beau tried to muster his men for yet another charge, and Lance Corporal Key thought him at once courageous and insane.

His own powder was wet, his hands frozen by the chilling rains, and loading his rifle in a prone position with numb fingers wasn't working.

His shoes were caked with icy mud, his uniform was soaked, and with the penetrating cold he could feel the pain in his leg beginning to spread in ways that troubled him.

He prayed for the rains to stop, and the sunshine and warmth to return.

He prayed for the end of battle.

At Union headquarters near the Four Corners just north of the mountain, General Protection Fault gathered his regimental commanders around a large though incomplete map of Byte Mountain and the surrounding area.

Reconnaissance reports did little to fill in critical and strategic areas of the map, let alone Confederate troop strengths on the crest and sides of the mountain fortress. General Fault was irritated with such gaps in the knowledge at his command.

His nemesis and old West Point war college colleague, General Jaylord Windows, had captured and secured Byte Mountain through a brilliant lightning strike in the middle of the night, outflanking General Fault in a most daring stratagem.

General Windows selected as his field headquarters the very peak of the mountain for its commanding and imposing vista of the surrounding region.

The southern flank of the mountain, comprising the expanse of the farms of Jeremy Doss and Edward M. Hertz, was crisscrossed by a network of roads, with one in particular, Alta Oak Lane, leading partway up the mountain itself.

Due to the rough and rocky terrain, this sector was well under the control of just two Confederate squads and would give protected passage to the southern army should retreat ever be a necessity.

General Windows looked down upon superior numbers of Union forces with not a little satisfaction.

Lt. Colonel Thomas N. Haardrive, commanding the embattled 67th Virginia Rifle Brigade along the lower perimeter, held the first line of defense against Fault's Army of the Potomac.

Ruthless in reputation, Haardrive was devilishly cruel with his own troops. Nicknamed "Crash Haardrive" by men serving under him, he drove them with unrelenting and unmerciful intensity, and numerous were those who slipped off into the night, deserting the cause that once brought them to stand for their country within a country.

Disillusioned, cold, and hungry, and no longer willing to accept the abuse of their superiors, hundreds left in this way, slipping into the darkness of night.

゠   ゠   ゠

Along the upper stony ridges, just below Chancellor's Break, Major General James B. Virhus held the second line of defense, commanding the combined 43rd Regiment of South Carolina and the 17th of Tennessee.

Virhus was a third-generation immigrant from Europe, following in the footsteps of his father and great uncle, both former officers in the Prussian army.

Virhus had graduated second in his class at West Point, a year following Generals Fault and Windows. He was intelligent and quick-witted, gifted in managing minute details in assessing the strength of the enemy, and skillful in strategic maneuvers under the heat of battle.

His was the plan followed by General Windows in the taking of

Byte Mountain twenty days prior. But Major General Virhus was by nature a loner, prone to bouts of crippling depression that affected his judgment at times.

His acerbic and biting tongue played havoc and wore heavily on his underlings, men of the line carefully avoiding all direct encounters with the man.

Corporal Mack Entossh of the 43rd South Carolina Regiment knew well his commanding officer's vitriol. Being originally from Boston, and unfairly maligned as a northerner at heart, he was the undeserved recipient of much of Virhus's angry tirades since his enlistment.

It was he who, in the heat of the fierce battle at C. Daniel Rhom's farmhouse, in an instance of unbridled rage engendered by the callous and ill-tempered general's abuse, sighted along his mountain rifle with deadly calm at a spot just behind Virhus's left ear and pulled the trigger.

≈ ≈ ≈

None were the wiser regarding how this loss came about, for it occurred at the height of confusion during pitched battle around the farmhouse.

A northern sharpshooter was credited with downing the major general. For his part, Corporal Entossh slipped silently into the darkness the next night and was gone, never to be heard of again.

The death of Major General Virhus represented a serious loss for General Windows and the Armies of the Confederacy.

≈ ≈ ≈

Challenged by the overwhelming numbers of the northern armies from the initial firing upon Fort Sumter, as well as by their superior armaments and firepower throughout the war, General Windows relied heavily upon skill and cunning in waging the South's argument against the Union.

Major General Virhus was especially deft with the slight of mind that confounded the likes of General Protection Fault, and his loss was not insubstantial.

General Windows selected a young officer from amongst his regimental commanders, one who had risen through the ranks, to succeed the deceased Virhus in carrying on the war for secession.

Major General Random A. Memory, uncle to Captain N. Sufficient Memory, himself a scholar of ancient battles while of wit but half that of his adversaries, was granted a field promotion on the nomination of his Commanding General because of his calm, dashing persona.

At midnight on Sunday the sixteenth of October, a night of the new moon, under the remnant clouds and scattered drizzles of a waning thunderstorm, General Protection Fault sent Lt. Ram Beau with four regiments of his finest sharpshooters and two regiments of cavalry in a pincer movement around Byte Mountain to secure its southern access.

❧   ❧   ❧

By 5 o'clock that morning, as the eastern skies slipped from the dark of night to the whisper of predawn light, Lt. Ram Beau had his men in place three hundred yards from the first line of Confederate defenses.

Corporal Icahn Mouus and Lance Corporal Key, sent as point guards to scout the Confederate sentries posted along the roads leading to the southern reaches of Byte Mountain, returned with word that sentries watched from but a few locations, the stretch of Alta Oak Lane leading to the mountain essentially unguarded.

Lt. Ram Beau stood in the dark next to a small outcropping of stone near Alta Oak Lane. He struck a match, shielding it from the elements. It flared momentarily and was swiftly extinguished, but its brief flame gave the agreed-upon signal to engage the enemy.

With the pounding hooves of the cavalry sounding like thunder unleashed, joined by the banshee wail of Corporal Mouus, a Virginian who elected to serve the Union opposite his brother, the Union forces struck quickly and decisively, sowing terror in an enemy rudely aroused from slumber.

Lt. Ram Beau led the two regiments of cavalry in a direct charge up Alta Oak Lane, breaching the first line of sleeping defenders and driving toward the redoubts dug into the upper reaches of Byte Mountain.

Captain U.P. Graade led the 34th and 39th Regiments of Massachusetts regulars in an assault across Hertz's farm against the right flank of the Confederate defensive line, while Lt. Keye Bord led the charge of the two Pennsylvania Light Rifle Brigades, the 7th and the 28th, against the Confederate left flank.

The din and fury of the assault washed over the sleeping Confederate soldiers, awakening them to the sudden shock that their positions had been overrun.

There was madness in the scramble for weapons in the dark, as the frightened men attempted to rally under the wave of soldiers in blue. Dense smoke spewed out of a hundred muskets all around as cries and screams split the air.

Lt. Bord's 28th Brigade struck the Confederates on their left flank with sudden fury, cutting down nearly a quarter of the sleepy defenders in their initial volley.

As the Rebel defenders under Capt. Robert E. Mail rallied to return fire, the 7th Brigade under Lt. Bord let loose a withering volley into the confused midst, the 28th quickly reloading.

Men in grey and homespun dropped in their tracks, killed

outright or severely wounded. The remaining men and boys tried in vain to return fire, but soon their numbers and will faded, and they abandoned their weapons and surrendered.

Meanwhile, Capt. Graade's two regiments of Massachusetts regulars slammed into the defensive line on their left. The Confederate right flank had heard the sounds of Lt. Ram Beau's cavalry charge as it carried the center of the defensive line, as well as the clatter of muskets coming from their own left flank.

In the first few minutes following the initial clash, Lt. P.C. Monitor led the defending Southerners in a wild and energetic effort to repel Graade's men, much to the latter's surprise, but Lt. Monitor's defense was too little and too late.

The sustained firing by the 34th and 39th Massachusetts regulars, coupled with their superior arms, quickly overwhelmed the troops of Southern defenders and brought them to their knees.

Acrid smoke obscured much of the battlefield as the fighting waned and the firing ceased.

Then all was silence but for the cries and whimpers of the dying, a sound wrenching on the ear.

*　　⸙　　⸙　　⸙*

The first rays of the rising sun touched the summit of Byte Mountain before reaching Hertz's farm at its foot.

General Windows was in receipt of communications from his commanders defending the southern perimeters of the mountain that the battle of Alta Oak Lane had been lost, and southern access to the mountain was now under the control of Union troops.

Byte Mountain was completely surrounded by the enemy, and all avenues of escape denied. General Windows considered circumstances facing his command, and solemnly called his regimental staff together.

Byte Mountain, while not a major pressing point in the South's war against the Union, was nevertheless a matter of pride in the scale of battles won and lost. This was a major loss.

General Windows addressed his commanders in subdued grave tones, expressing his gratitude and pride, and that of the South, for their courageous efforts in their lost cause.

The loss of Byte Mountain would go down in history as an embarrassment for Robert E. Lee and the South, but General Windows wanted to ensure that his staff knew it was of his doing, not due to any lack on their part.

By mid-morning, through an emissary under a flag of truce, with a mind toward minimizing the further loss of men under his command, General Jaylord Windows petitioned General Protection Fault of the Army of the Potomac "for the honorable surrender of the troops under my command, the Armies of Virginia, South Carolina, and Tennessee..."

In the lazy early afternoon of October 17th, storm clouds now dissipated, the sun warming the flanks of Byte Mountain, Lance Corporal Key sat on the lip of the ridge overlooking the Shenandoah Valley.

The smoke of battle was now cleared, aided by a gentle wind blowing from the south, the sounds of guns stilled. He felt warmth returning to his leg once again.

He drew a wrinkled slip of paper from his blouse pocket, and taking the stub of a pencil, dabbed it on the end of his tongue and set to writing a letter to his father in Gettysburg...

The Window on Midnight

The old wooden planks burned under her feet as she flew down the length of the rickety old pier, the sun blazing down, her ponytail trailing out behind her in the heavy sultry air.

Her one thought was to catch air in the leap from the end of the pier, throwing herself hell-bent into space, fighting gravity even though for only the briefest of moments. Her right foot slammed hard onto the third plank from the end, sending a jolt up her lithe body.

The uncoiling of her leg muscle thrust her body up to the sky. She aimed high, for the sun, arms thrown above her head, her legs continuing to run on the air, digging for advantage—she was airborne.

Jenn rose into the air, her eyes ever on the prize, her body atop an Atlas booster lifting off the cape.

The roar of silence was deafening in her ears, inner vibrations on the verge of pain shaking her down to her toes, the electric charge in the ether lifting and filling her heart. And in that moment, suspended at the apex of the arc, space and time melded into one and time stood still—she was free of the bonds of earth.

The roar of the engines was deafening, and the powerful throbbing washed over her body in a torrent. Jenn grabbed the open metal ribbing of the aircraft fuselage to steady herself as freezing winds whipped through the open machine gunports.

Jenn brushed her ponytail back over her shoulder. Looking to her side, she came face-to-face with a woman draped in a dark lavender and blue cloak, her blue-green eyes gleaming in the semi-darkness of the plane's interior. She smiled and put her hand on Jenn's shoulder. Above the thunder of engines and the chill whipping of winds there was a faint static crackling, all but lost in the din.

"...(crackle)...th...ish...S...arl...(crackle)..." The radioman hunched over his console, his hand holding the earpiece tightly to his ear, listening for anything coming over the airways, his fatigued mind hearing nothing. His eyelids drooped; his head nodded forward.

"What's happening?" asked Jenn, shouting over the noise.

"This is the last of several patrol planes returning from a reconnaissance flight over enemy territory," whispered the woman. Jenn was surprised that she could hear the woman clearly even though she whispered. "They develop the film in minutes, and squadrons of bombers take off before sunrise with photographs of strategic targets deep within the enemy's territories. Then, reconnaissance planes take off again the next night for more of the same."

Silence. Jenn stirred, disturbed by something in the background, something almost missed in the drone of the four powerful engines.

"What's that noise?" she asked.

"His radio isn't working, though he doesn't know it," whispered the woman. "He doesn't hear anything but static—atmospheric conditions are affecting his reception. The garbled message we hear is a challenge from a naval ship on the sea's surface below for the aircraft to identify itself."

"But if they don't hear it..." Jenn's question trailed off, her eyes fixed on the man listening to static and hearing nothing.

The first explosion came without warning just to the left of the aircraft, a red and orange violent burst, a telltale black blossom illuminated for just a moment from within. The shock waves tossed those near slumber onto the floor, throwing the plane about as though it were a rag doll.

The plane's wings shuddered, the fuselage groaning under the impact of the near hit. A second explosion followed immediately below them, pieces of metal tearing through the outer skin of the large plane. "Up and at 'em, guys! We've got bogeys planting roses out there and we don't know where the hell they are!" shouted the captain over the intercom. The third explosion was deafening, the concussion violent and rending, filling the aircraft with flames and acrid smoke and flying debris.

Flames licked up the sidewalls as electrical wires flashed and sparks flew all about, filling the interior with the smell of ozone. "Anyone see who's firing on us?" yelled the captain, his voice straining against the chaos and noise.

"I don't see a thing, sir," yelled the copilot.

"Shit—help me with this, Mac!" yelled the captain, struggling with the controls. The airmen throughout the aircraft worked feverishly extinguishing flames, also tending to those wounded and still alive.

"Goddammit, guys! Give me damage reports!" shouted the captain. "Give me something!" The lights in the aft section blinked and sizzled, then failed, plunging everything into darkness except for illumination from the fires.

"Captain, engine three is on fire, and it looks like number one is trailing black smoke," shouted the copilot, reaching to cut the fuel to the two engines and feathering both props to decease any drag.

≈   ≈   ≈

"Can't we do anything?" whispered Jenn, tension gripping her body.

"There's nothing we can do," replied the woman. "This happened a very long time ago, its course already once played out."

Jenn looked into her companion's eyes with a puzzled expression. Her hold on the plane's ribbing tightened, knuckles turning white under the pressure as she steadied herself.

A fourth explosion ripped through the tail section of the plane, and the aircraft lurched to the right, rolling over and descending a thousand feet before the captain could right her and bring her course level again.

"Murphy! Come to me—tell me what's happening back there!" shouted the captain.

(crackle, crackle) "Un, Conley here, Captain—Murphy's dead... the fire's pretty bad back here, sir, and—mmph, my goddam leg's busted up pretty good—I don't think I can get out."

The captain grit his teeth. "Hold on, Conley—I'll get someone back there!" (crackle, sizzle)

"Mansfield, sir—Roberts is working on the hydraulic lines— they're really smashed up, sir—there's oil all over..." (crackle, crackle)

"Have Roberts go back and help Conley," shouted the captain. The wing struts creaked and groaned under the high stress maneuvering as pilot and copilot struggled to keep the aircraft flying. The noise was deafening.

"Baker here—we've got a shitload of trouble, sir—a whole chunk of the tail section is gone—I'm looking out into a black sky!" Static followed, and then the intercom went dead.

"Shit! Sparks! Get that radio working again—I have to know what's happening!"

"I'll do my best, Captain!" Smoke began to fill the cockpit, and the captain threw open the side window to clear the air, copilot following suit.

⥱ ⥱ ⥱

The wind whipped in through the open windows, blowing everything not tied down into the air but only clearing some of the smoke. (crackle...sizzzzle...crackle) Then, "I think I've got it, Captain!" shouted the radioman.

"Renfrow here, sir (crackle)—Pendleton is hurt real bad—oh shit—goddammit, I can't get the bleeding to stop—I can't do it, sir!—Ohh, I'm sorry...! O god, help me...!"

The flames in the cockpit rose higher, eating away at the insulation on the wires running along the ceiling and under the floorboards, searing the aluminum metal surfaces on the instrument panel. The copilot directed the extinguisher at the base of the flames, but to no avail—the flames were everywhere and continued stubbornly to rage out of control.

⥱ ⥱ ⥱

A fifth explosion ripped through the belly of the aircraft, sending a violent shudder through the length of the plane, but somehow she stayed in the air.

The captain struggled with the controls as the plane lurched to one side. The controls were frozen, nothing responding to his or the copilot's efforts. The gauges flicked back and forth or were dead, giving no reading of the plane's operations. Smoke now filled the cockpit, choking the captain and his copilot, their eyes burning from the sting of smoke.

Fires burned everywhere—the captain shouted into the

intercom, "Aw damn! Out, everyone get the hell out! I can't keep her up anymore! She's going down!"

The whine of the two remaining engines filled the air, the bellowing of a bull elephant in its death throes—the aircraft slid onto its side, slipping over into its final descent toward the seascape and darkness below.

∿   ∿   ∿

"Why did you bring me here?" asked Jenn quietly as she watched the final seconds of the aircraft's fall. "Why to this place, to these men?"

The woman gave a sideways glance, her eyes steady, deep, calm. "The navigator on board this plane was your grandfather." Silence.

Jenn's eyes closed slightly as she turned to the woman in puzzlement. "My grandfather was reported missing in action," she whispered, half to herself but also to the woman. "His plane was lost off the coast of North Africa, whereabouts unknown," she added.

"Missing in action, yes, but whereabouts not unknown," said the woman gently.

The two stood without speaking for a long while, their eyes holding each other's gaze as the scene before them grew dim in the twilight of early morning. "Who knew?" Jenn finally asked.

Silence. Then, "The men of the USS Elizabeth Freeman," came the reply.

∿   ∿   ∿

The splash cleared her head, and Jenn relaxed as the buoyancy of the water slowed her descent below the surface.

Reaching up and cupping her hands, she pulled down with powerful strokes against the liquid surrounding her, sliding upward through the cool water, eyes wide open—she could see the surface approaching.

As she burst through the membrane separating two worlds, emerging into the realm of air, she drew in a deep breath that filled her lungs—what a delicious feeling.

She was alive. She was home.

The Lavender Baron

His parents liked his brother best. He was taller, had that dark handsome look about him, and was smarter than Hans.

Manfred von Richthofen graduated at the head of his class with honors, and when he enlisted in the budding Army Air Service his parents were so proud.

Hans, on the other hand, struggled and had a mediocre existence as a student, returning home upon graduation to join the family business as an apprentice silversmith. He was skilled with his hands, exhibiting an untrained artistic bent.

His workmanship went far beyond anything Herr von Richthofen had achieved in all his forty years as a master silversmith. Hans reluctantly accepted the praise he began to garner with his artistic work, but he was unhappy. He spent long days in the workshop of the family business, but his heart just wasn't in it.

He was in a place far away—soaring, a homing pigeon amongst majestic eagles in flight.

He dreamed of flying, of being cut from the bounds of earthly ties, of lifting into the air unfettered by the pull of gravity.

Flying was still quite new in the world, although the thought of flight had teased man from time immemorial. Hans was one so teased, and he ached for the opportunity to ease that ache with flight.

Manfred von Richthofen, dubbed the Red Baron because of the red cowling on the Fokker Dr.I he flew, quickly learned the skills to put his wood and silk eagle through incredible paces, and in early encounters with British and American airmen caused considerable consternation with his aerial antics.

One rarely was wounded in those early bouts, mainly because of poor marksmanship with a pistol held outside the cockpit or aimed into the wind.

Baron von Richthofen was a superior marksman on the pistol range, but buffeting winds, the open cockpit, and the uncertainty in early flying machines resulted in fly-by shootings with nary a hit.

Early machine guns were mounted on the upper wings of biplanes to avoid shooting up one's own propeller, and were most difficult to aim.

One day, an aircraft designer mounted a machine gun on the engine housing of a flying machine, synchronizing it to shoot through a fully rotating propeller. One's aim improved significantly, and the odds in the exchange of gunfire in the air shot up considerably.

Hans loved to hear Manfred tell of his aerial escapades, and was glad for him. But he was sorely jealous, and wished that he, too, could lift off into the wild blue skies.

Manfred, for his part, loved his brother deeply, and wished he had a chance to climb into the cockpit of a flying machine, watching for any opportunity.

Then, during a particularly hazardous sortie over the French countryside, his friend and fellow pilot Karl Miller, seeking to escape the pursuit of a hotshot American pilot, flew his Fokker D.V around a stand of trees and into the side of a barn, killing him instantly.

The squadron leader began the search among new recruits to fill the position left by Miller's death.

Manfred gave his superior his brother's name, saying he was a highly skilled craftsman of the air. A wild exaggeration, that.

Hans was pleased when his brother told of him being considered to take the new and more powerful Fokker D.VII, replacing Miller. He would be joining his brother in the air.

Manfred smiled and said, "You will be a fine airman."

Hans shook his head. "I do not know the first thing about a flying machine," he stammered to Manfred.

"Do not worry, little brother. I will show you with my flying machine."

Morning sunlight peeked over the treetops of the Black Forest as two figures huddled against the cold on the field of the aerodrome. They walked to the front of the lone aircraft sitting on the grassy field, and the taller of the two motioned the other into the cockpit.

Manfred instructed Hans in the controls of his flying machine. Once the ignition switch was on the Red Baron threw his weight onto the broad propeller, pulling downward with one swift movement and stepping deftly aside.

The plane coughed and belched a plume of blue-grey smoke out the exhausts. Then, with a sputter building into a roar, the engine caught.

Manfred motioned for Hans to move the throttle forward, and

the throbbing of the engine smoothed into a mesmerizing purr, climbing a scale higher.

Manfred removed the blocks holding the wheels, slipped under the wing and climbed onto the trailing edge, lifting himself into the cockpit behind his brother.

Hans's eyes were open wide, the excitement burning in them just slightly tinged with fear.

✈   ✈   ✈

Under the calm and sure eyes of his brother, Hans moved the throttle ahead, the massive propeller driving the flying machine forward. Hans guided the aircraft along a grassy field to the head of the runway. Without a pause he thrust the throttle forward, holding on for dear life.

The engine roared like a wounded animal, driving the wooden and silk apparition down the runway. After a mere eighty feet it lifted into the air.

Hans's eyes filled with tears as he pulled back on the joystick, and the flying machine climbed steeply, every part of it vibrating violently. Hans looked over the edge of the cockpit—the ground was so far below, the trees so tiny from up here.

Manfred smiled.

✈   ✈   ✈

Hans repeated this routine every day for a month, Manfred's orange Fokker Dr.I with a red cowling lumbering briefly down the runway and lifting into the air to climb upward in a long, lazy spiral until the flying machine drew level with the clouds. Up there, Hans could see almost forever.

His flying machine flew as the birds, with the wind beneath its wings.

Hans learned quickly, and Manfred was most impressed and proud. His brother was becoming a fine pilot and would soon wear the wings of the feared Flying Circus.

One day, the squadron leader approached and asked Manfred to tell Hans he wanted to see him. Hans was excited, almost as much as Manfred.

The two brothers arrived at the headquarters building at the aerodrome, where Hans was formally invited to join the flying squadron.

Once he accepted they led him out onto the field, where a brand-new Fokker D.VII sat, fresh paint shining in the early morning light.

The new flying machine had green and orange markings, white square patches on each end of the upper wing filled with the black German cross. The cowling over the powerful engine was a distinctive light purple.

Manfred laughed and dubbed Hans the Lavender Baron. Hans beamed with pride, chuckling with his brother.

Dark clouds were scattered across an early morning sky when the call came for the members of the Flying Circus to take on their most dangerous mission yet.

Manfred knew that the British and American fliers would be up in large numbers, and he worried for Hans, who was still a green recruit. Flying practice sorties over the lush fields of the Rhine Valley was one thing—the stakes today were considerably higher.

Before he climbed into his aircraft, he threw an arm across Hans's shoulders and wished him luck and good hunting. Hans returned the wish and climbed into his flying machine. He sat back and threw his silk scarf around his neck. It was time.

The air at the higher altitudes was freezing cold, and Hans clapped his gloved hands together to warm them.

Manfred had warned him to wear his long underwear, and he was glad for the brotherly advice. The drone of the powerful engine drowned out all sounds—otherwise, Hans was sure the other fliers would hear his teeth chattering.

Hans glanced over to his left and waved to the Red Baron. Through the brisk thin air, Manfred smiled back.

Hans caught movement out of the corner of his eye, and saw Manfred waving his arms, pointing up and to the west. Hans followed the direction of his gesturing and saw the glint of sun off something metallic high above him.

Gun metal, thought Hans. *Oh, man!*

He tightened his grip on the joystick and pulled back slightly. The nose of his flying machine came up, pointing toward the flight of aircraft bound in his direction.

Suddenly, the whine of high velocity bullets filled the air around him, and Hans heard the fabric of his aircraft taking hits.

Hans pulled sharply to his right and rolled over, rising hard up into the sun.

As he came out of his roll, he saw the blue-grey coloring of a Spad flying machine flash by him, the Hat in the Ring insignia of the 94th Aero Pursuit Squadron on its side.

Hans's blood ran cold, fear seizing his mind. These were the fliers of the American Air Service led by Eddie Rickenbacker. He'd heard a lot about them.

Again, he heard the buzz of bullets whistling around him, and again he pulled up and over, then into a steep dive, spiraling downward with the ground rushing up at him.

He heaved with all his might on the joystick and pulled out of his dive just twenty feet off the ground. Looking back, Hans saw the blue-grey Spad still on his tail.

The way the pursuer was glued to him, Hans knew it was the hotshot American pilot, Terry Newby. Newby was a cocky young flier, born in California but raised in Texas. He was bigger than life, with a dark side to his personality that came out in spades.

Skilled with words and gifted with a superior intellect, Newby used a cutting tongue in his dealings with everyone. His best friend and fellow pilot, Jack Burrows, was also a Californian, but raised in the rural outbacks of Oregon. He was an introvert with the social skills of a rock.

Newby's and Burrows's skills in the air, however, were astounding. They flew as though the wood and silk of their aircraft were the sinews and feathers of their arms and shoulders.

They anticipated their adversaries in ways a human couldn't or shouldn't—and appeared in places that weren't possible. Yet there they were.

Between them they had thirteen kills to their names, and it was still early in the war.

Hans knew when Newby was around, Burrows wasn't very far away.

⥺   ⥺   ⥺

Hans could hear the faint chatter of a 50mm machine gun above the roar of his own engine. He throttled full up and pushed his flying machine toward a bank of clouds.

Suddenly, he heard metal striking metal, and a tremendous pain shot through his body. The cockpit filled with black smoke as the engine began to sputter.

Hans could see a thin streak of black oil spurting out from the side of the engine compartment. His left side was numb, and he had difficulty lifting his arms to control the joystick.

Then, a red flying machine flew dangerously close right between Hans and the American, forcing the pursuer to pull up to avoid a mid-air collision. As the blue-grey flying machine rose and passed in front of the Red Baron, Hans struggled and pulled into a momentary stall, coming around just in time to see Manfred falling in behind the American pilot.

Now the Red Baron was the pursuer, the American the pursued.

Manfred fired his two machine guns with deadly accuracy, hitting his target just behind the propeller and raking it full along the side.

The American slumped forward, and his aircraft slipped into a dive toward the ground below, trailing a thin but growing streak of black smoke.

❖ ❖ ❖

Hans's flying machine fluttered like a bird struck by pellets and began a slow spiraling descent toward the ground below. Hans's left arm was useless, and he was too weak to manage the controls.

Manfred followed his brother's crippled airship down, watching as it gained speed and slammed violently into the side of a hill.

Shaken, but now angered, he began climbing once again and rejoined the combat with the British and American fliers.

The Red Baron pulled in behind the blue-grey Spad of Burrows, and playing with his cocky opponent fired a burst that weakened the enemy's wing structure.

Burrows winced on seeing the damage to his aircraft. His eyes grew wider as the pursuing avenger stayed on his tail despite all efforts to shake him off.

The Red Baron fired another long burst, this time hitting the engine and propeller of the American's aircraft. The plane began to shudder and wobble violently, Burrows struggling to keep the crippled flying machine in the air.

Manfred watched as Burrows pulled frantically on the joystick, smiling as flames began to eat away at the silk around the engine housing. He followed the crippled and burning aircraft as it spiraled down out of the clouds.

Just as the blue-grey Spad approached the crest of a hill, Manfred fired one final burst of his dual machine guns into the dying aircraft, watching as it exploded on impact with the ground.

"That was for Hans," he whispered through his teeth.

The Red Baron pulled out of his deadly pursuit and brought his eagle up into the sun.

He climbed in a long lazy spiral upward, until the flying machine came level with the clouds and he could see almost forever.

Hans's flying machine had touched the clouds, and he now flew as the birds, with the wind beneath his wings...

The Day the Universe Tilted

"It is told there is a man in Padua who has created a most wondrous scientific instrument," said the old traveler.

"It is so," said his traveling companion matter-of-factly, "but it was not in Padua—it was Venice."

"Hmmm, so it was," replied the old traveler, remembering.

Midday sunlight beat down on the two as they made their way along the dusty road. The winds had long since died down, leaving the air heavy and oppressive, giving no respite to the weary pair.

"It is told the man has made the eye to see what is far distant as if it were before him," said the old traveler, looking to his companion for confirmation.

"I have heard the same," came the reply.

"Is it to be believed?" asked the old traveler of the other.

His companion turned his eyes heavenward, and with a shrug of his shoulders said, "He who first told me swears by his mother's grave that it is so."

"Then I, too, will say it is so," said the old traveler, a slight smile on the corners of his lips, his pupils deep pools of onyx.

⁂

Darkness shrouded one side of the giant mirror as it hurtled silently along its travels, its solar panels spread like the wings of a giant albatross spanning ten meters tip to tip, capturing the prevailing solar rays on its lonely journey through space.

The space mirror's trajectory was intended to carry it past the planet's sunlit surface at an altitude of 60 million kilometers, past the terminator into synchronous orbit over the polar regions, providing maximum view of the planet's magnificent rings.

The immense mirror was programmed to capture the phases of the planet's rings, waxing and waning from a full-on panorama through the sliver of the on-edge view, twice in the span of a single orbit of thirty Earth days.

Mankind from time immemorial has been drawn to the transformation of celestial bodies that, like the moon, pass through ordered phases, beginning in primordial darkness and rising through ever increasing increments to the fullness of the lunar reflected lightness, then through the cycle of its decline into darkness once again. It heralds possibilities—the promise of birth and life, death and once again rebirth—and touches an ancient longing someplace deep within.

The celestial eyes of the night wink, a flirtatious gesture from the bounds of the heavens, and man is always smitten. It has ever been thus.

✼   ✼   ✼

The old traveler bent over his evening meal as his companion tended the fire. "You travel to Venice, my friend?"

"Yes, I am to visit with the master scientist himself."

"Oh?" responded the elder traveler, a curious twinkle in his eyes.

"Yes—I travel at the behest of the Archduke of the Hapsburg

Court. This scientific instrument is of great interest to his generals."

"Ah," said the elder traveler, nodding as his eyes filled with sadness.

"You take exception to my mission?"

"No, not to your mission," said the elder traveler, a melancholy smile on his lips, "since it falls within the business margins of those who make wars. It is just that our generals look to scientists for weapons used in the waging of wars and take little note of the price extracted by such ventures."

"Hmmm," sighed the younger man aloud. "It is always thus, I am afraid."

"Yes," the elder agreed, nodding again. The two then sat in silence as the stars above listened.

Signals beamed across millions of miles of space maintained the Galileo Surveyor spacecraft aligned along the axis of the broadcast from mission control, keeping the mirror's dish oriented toward the approaching planet. The onboard computer had long since locked the space traveler on two other solar system markers, the Sun and Neptune.

Computer readouts at mission control confirmed that the mirror was focused full-face toward the approaching ringed planet. Dr. Julian Goodman, co-director of the Galileo Surveyor's exploration of Saturn, watched as the computer image of the approaching planet began to take shape. A rousing cheer rose from the technicians and scientists in the mission control complex as the screen of darkness cleared and there appeared an amazing sight.

"Can you work the resolution of that image, Stefanie?" asked Dr. Goodman across the banks of computers.

"I'm on it," said Stefanie. Dr. Stefanie Purehardt was Galileo Surveyor co-director and project coordinator, also the nominal genius behind the project in Dr. Goodman's eyes. The image onscreen was of a bright crescent, with a diagonal mixture of light and shadow bisecting its face—the rings seen from on-edge.

"Stefanie, fix that orientation," uttered Dr. Goodman. "Please..."

"I'm on it," replied Stefanie, tapping a series of codes on the keyboard. The image onscreen rotated until the line of the rings appeared as a horizontal line across the planet's partial face.

"Thank you," said Dr. Goodman.

"Why'd you do that, Dr. Goodman?" asked a young man seated at console #47.

"It's always a little distracting to view something not on either a north-south or east-west axis," he answered. "Artistically, I personally prefer the diagonal, something off-center," he continued, "but for our purposes here, technically we should keep things on a proper grid."

"What does he mean, artistically?" asked the young man quietly of Stefanie.

"Dr. Goodman views what we're seeing as an artistic expression of the universe. He sometimes just likes to look at the images, not as a composite of digital impulses, but an expression of some truth that is out there."

"Ah."

⸽   ⸽   ⸽

"The truth is that we are steady and unmoving at the center of the universe," said the young traveler matter-of-factly. "This scientist speaks of a universe where the Earth moves about the Sun," he added with a derisive chuckle.

"This man has spoken thus, I believe," said the elder man.

192

"As a scientist, he must be exceptional to have discovered an aid for seeing long distances—but, in matters of Holy Writ, he is clearly out of his depth," said the younger.

"Perhaps."

"These words of his have caused quite a stir in the Holy City!" added the younger man, growing more intense. "He should restrict his explorations to the tides and the workings of clocks."

"Ah, he should be so wise," responded the elder traveler thoughtfully. "It is reported the Cardinal Tomaso Nellusone called upon him at his home, asking that he recant his publicly stated belief. He is stubborn and bullheaded, this man—he refused."

"He is that, and foolhardy!" said the younger man.

"Yes," the elder agreed, nodding. "Cardinal Jamasini Bertoni has called a tribunal at the Medici Court for the end of this month."

"I believe the Pontiff Jassui Gaeyuordini and the whole of the Holy City will watch these proceedings with much interest."

"Indeed they will," responded the elder, "as will I."

≥   ≥   ≥

Preliminary review of images received from the Galileo Surveyor probe from Saturn produced images promising significant materials for study and analysis in the coming months. Dr. Purehardt credited the quality of the images to the dedicated work of the technical crew, the state-of-the-art hardware for the endeavor, and a dollop of pure and simple luck. She kept a small figurine of a leprechaun seated on a tree stump tipping his hat on the top of her console as homage to this latter element of the venture—one mustn't take anything for granted with NASA projects.

Dr. Purehardt observed the image onscreen, the whole crew watching in wonder at the events unfolding millions of miles distant. Dr. Goodman looked over to Dr. Purehardt and winked his approval. Dr. Purehardt smiled in return and turned back to the monitor screen.

⅌　⅌　⅌

The day was drawing to a close as the two travelers prepared themselves for the evening's respite. The Sun set across the wide valley, seeming momentarily to pause at the lip of the mountains to the west before slipping beyond the darkened ridge. The two men sat and watched in silence as twilight drew close around them.

"I suppose this scientist will plead innocence," said the younger traveler.

"I do not know. He is very stubborn, and may not consider the implications of his position."

"You do not believe he is correct in stating that the Sun is the center of our universe?" asked the young man, a wry smile crossing his lips.

"Oh, I believe he is stating his beliefs on the matter," responded the elder traveler quietly, avoiding answering the young man directly. "He makes a persuasive argument for his views."

The elder traveler sighed and looked to the distant heavens. "Do you see that light in the firmament just above the hills to the north? Beyond those hills lies the Holy City—that light, my friend, portends something momentous in our times."

The young man followed the elder's pointing finger to the tiny light in the sky. "How do you know this?" queried the young man.

"It is in the stars, my young friend—it is in the stars," indicated the elder, his voice but a whisper.

And just for a moment the young man thought he felt the Earth move.

The Untouchables

It was a dark and miserable night. The cold nor'wester coming in off the Great Lakes brought the chill to minus forty degrees, keeping everyone indoors. It was the worst February in anyone's memory, and everyone complained bitterly.

The cold wintry streets of Chicago, carrying the lifeblood of the city, also openly carried the liquid gold of the mob in the form of moonshine whiskey.

Hundreds of speakeasies throughout the city continued to do a thriving business in the distilled form of the second forbidden fruit, despite prohibition and the efforts of the feds to eliminate alcohol for sale.

Local politicians and police alike turned a blind eye to the goings on, receiving into their eager hands a portion of the wealth of nations.

Albatross Capon, Al Capon to friends, head of the Chicago syndicate, ran a ruthless operation, stopping at nothing to increase the reach of his power and influence.

Capon's second in command was Tommy the Buzzard, a.k.a. Tommy-Gun Nesslan, an introverted and cantankerous loner, whose tongue cut any who opposed him to pieces with machine gun–like precision.

Ruthless he was, and nasty to a fault. He delighted in causing pain, and always slept soundly at night. It was rumored his mother, to toughen his hide, used to bathe him by dunking him in a tub of vinegar, holding him by his left ankle. Most everyone rejected this as urban myth, though any experience of his unbridled anger proved he was indeed full of piss and vinegar. Such irony.

Capon's syndicate was held together and fed in part by the austere and stranglehold business sense of Gimpy Jimmy Bortun, a.k.a. Jimmy the Beak, a squint-eyed keeper of the books, whose heart (so it was said) had been left in San Francisco, along with the body parts of all the bird-brained idiots who had dared to cross him.

He could stop a falcon at thirty paces with the glance of his one good eye, and many were they who crossed that one eye and died regretting it.

Jimmy the Beak was a perfect partner for Tommy the Buzzard, for they both held true to the first principle of their dark profession—never give a sucker an even break.

And they didn't.

The streets of Chicago ran red with the blood of their enemies, and the local police commissioner turned a deaf ear to these goings on, being richly rewarded for his selective inattention.

Nary a week went by without local newspaper headlines citing the death of a gangster who crossed Al Capon, or the suspicious accident of someone who failed to make payment on his debt to Jimmy the Beak. Particularly memorable was the story of a finch whose jaw was broken because she flinched when Tommy-Gun Nesslon walked into the dining room at the Astoria.

The playing of such deadly games lay heavily on the Windy City, and the war between the gangland families began to wear thin on all but the local police.

❧   ❧   ❧

The director of the FBI—the Federal Bird Investigators—was J. Edgar Hoopoe.

Now, J. Edgar Hoopoe was one strange bird—a loner by disposition, mean-spirited by choice, and given to strange tastes in clothing with a fetish involving feathers and silk panties.

J. Edgar Hoopoe was also a very angry bird, feared by those on the darker side of the law and loathed equally by those in his service who failed to meet his expectations in the execution of their duties.

He was a short stout bird, with a big beak—the better for poking into other people's business, he said. He said this often, believing himself funny in those instances, but he had no sense of humor. People laughed, but neither at him nor with him.

J. Edgar Hoopoe was utterly ruthless in his pursuit of the criminal mind, a stickler for even the most obscure of regulations and a workaholic given to twenty-hour workdays.

He was mindful of those minute details that led eventually to the failure of the criminal mind, and he carried his war to the likes of Al Capon with a decided vengeance.

❧   ❧   ❧

J. Edgar Hoopoe's top agent, Elliot Nest, had come up through the ranks and established the reputation of being seagull tenacious, deadly serious with an aggressive streak, and thoroughly knowl-edgeable of the underworld and the ways of wise guys.

Elliot Nest's assistants were Tony Robinni, an Italian American boxer who'd grown up on the streets of the Bronx, and Johnny Sparrowski, an old-world Polish immigrant who had come to Chicago by way of the northern migration flyways.

Sparrowski was of the old school—you work hard, harder than the bad guys, and you treat them with the same shit and muck as they dish out, and if you get up early enough you get the worm before he gets you.

If you bend the law in the process, as long as you get the bad guy in the end you're doing it right.

Elliot Nest was aware of Sparrowski's reputation and held him in high regard.

For his own part, he had understood quickly that hesitation meant death, a lesson learned as he watched his partner die in the line of duty. Afterward he chose to shoot first and ask questions in the cleanup.

One of the things that Nest relished, which irritated the hell out of Capon, was to raid his speakeasies and smash his beer kegs and steins.

During one stretch of fifteen days in late November, Nest hit twenty-four of Capon's businesses, damaging property and dump-ing thousands of gallons of liquid gold, costing Capon thousands of dollars in fun and revenue.

In addition, Capon's reputation was being besmirched by the likes of a punk like Nest, and this didn't sit well with the Chicago kingpin in the least.

⸺ ⸺ ⸺

Johnny Sparrowski brought a legendary reputation to the bureau based on the fact that he had killed three of Capon's gang in a wild shoot-out behind one of Capon's speakeasies.

Capon was furious as hell. It is a dangerous thing to anger your enemy—revenge is a powerful motivator, and it can give one an edge in power. But Nest always assigned Sparrowski to any case involving suspected links with Capon, in part because Sparrowski was his best agent, but also because it stuck it in the eye of the surly gangster.

Capon had lost his second in command on that bleak Sunday, one Blackie Byrd, a wild psychopathic hitbird with a suspected kill list of thirteen, and two mindless crownies from Philadelphia.

Capon was furious and totally beside himself that his men were unable to get these federal agents off his back. He cursed the day Elliot Nest was hatched, and with a vow to evening the score with his old nemesis began secretly plotting his revenge.

Early on a Sunday evening, Johnny Sparrowski was driving down Fifth Avenue when he noticed a sleek black sedan behind him. When he turned, the sleek black sedan followed; when he stopped for a signal, the sleek black sedan stopped well behind him.

Sparrowski caught on quickly, and radioed headquarters that he was being tailed. He was sure it was Capon's men, although he couldn't see their beaks. He suspected Tommy the Buzzard was behind the wheel because of the erratic driving. Jimmy the Beak was likely riding shotgun.

Elliot Nest spoke over the speaker: "Sparrowski, keep driving as though nothing's the matter. Take a left on Lakeside Drive, then head past the harbor master's station toward the landing at Moss Beach."

Nest's voice began to crackle, getting lost in the canyon of tall buildings. Sparrowski tapped the radio, trying to clear up the reception, but he was nearly out of range of the headquarters' transmitters.

"Oh, shit!" muttered Sparrowski, half to himself.

Nest stood over his radioman as the crackling sounded at headquarters. "Oh, shit!" he muttered, half to himself.

"Robinni!" chirped Nest. "Get down to Moss Beach right away and give Sparrowski backup—and take the big guns!"

Tony Robinni quickly left headquarters, heading south on the expressway toward Moss Beach.

Sparrowski turned left past the last warehouse building just south of the harbormaster's station and headed out on the dirt road toward the beach. The sleek black sedan following him kept a safe distance behind him, but there was no denying what was happening now.

Sparrowski slowed his sleek grey sedan as he neared the gravel landing that led to the water's edge. He stopped just short of the lapping waves and left the engine running and the lights on.

The car following him stopped, and Sparrowski could hear its engine idling, its lights still on. The two figures in the car didn't move.

Sparrowski reached in his jacket and unlatched the strap holding his 9mm Beretta. It felt warm to the touch as his hand slowly grasped the handle, his feather sliding into the trigger housing.

Still no movement from the other car. His eyes were open wide, unblinking, locked on the vehicle behind him.

Then, Sparrowski saw the passenger side door open and someone step out, protected by the car door. He tensed, slowly drew his automatic out of its holster and rested it lightly on his thigh, his eyes still scanning the scene behind.

Suddenly the figure ducked down, and Sparrowski could see it draw a large gun, the barrel leveled at the back of his head.

Sparrowski tensed, and in a movement of split timing hit the door handle, shoved against the door with his shoulder, and lunged out onto his shoulder and back, rolling in a ball to the water's edge.

At the same moment, shots rang out. Sparrowski could hear metal tearing into metal and glass where he had just been sitting.

Sparrowski came up with his 9mm Beretta blazing. He could hear his shots hitting the other car, metal again tearing into metal and glass—but this time also into feathers and flesh.

A scream came from the car as Sparrowski emptied his automatic with deadly accuracy.

Then, a sudden pain shot through his side, and he dropped his weapon. Grabbing at his shoulder, he rolled over behind his car.

He struggled to get up, but found that pain pinned him down. He could feel blood oozing out of the wound.

In the semi-darkness he heard footsteps coming toward him. There in the glare of his headlights stood Jimmy the Beak, blood soaking the feathers at his shoulder, a thin trickle flowing down his left side.

He was holding a very large gun in his right wing, pointing its long barrel at him.

Sparrowski struggled to reach for his 9mm, but remembered he had just emptied his clip. Besides, the pain in his shoulder stopped him—he winced and fell back.

Jimmy the Beak smiled as he steadied the very big gun, leveling it at Sparrowski's head.

Then, standing next to Jimmy the Beak Sparrowski saw Tommy the Buzzard. He, too, had a very large gun.

"Say your prayers, punk," sneered Tommy the Buzzard, and Sparrowski could see him begin to squeeze the trigger.

A loud explosion ripped through the air, and Tommy the Buzzard's body lurched to the side, his very big gun flying over his head.

A second explosion, and Jimmy the Beak grabbed at his neck. The force of the bullet threw him off his feet and onto the hood of Sparrowski's car.

As Jimmy the Beak's body slid off the hood and onto the gravel, Sparrowski saw coming out of the shadows into the glow of the headlights the familiar face of his partner, Tony Robinni. Robinni held a very large gun in his wing, its barrel still smoking. He smiled, holstered his piece, and knelt down beside the car where Sparrowski lay.

"You all right?" Robinni asked.

"I would be, if you'd get your ass in gear and take me to a hospital!" he chirped.

"Yeah, yeah!" Robinni replied, a gleam in his eyes and a smile on his beak. "Just like you to bitch right after I've saved your ass!"

⊰　⊰　⊰

Elliot Nest came by the hospital late one afternoon and found Sparrowski sitting on the side of his bed, his head still bandaged, his wing in a sling. He had dressed and was waiting for the doctor to sign his release. He was anxious to get back to work.

Nest congratulated him and his partner for taking out Capon's top two henchbirds. "You done good! Ole J. Edgar Hoopoe is putting you up for the Freedom Medal, Sparrowski. It's the highest honor that can be bestowed for heroism beyond the call of duty."

Sparrowski blinked his eyes and was embarrassed.

"And, just so's you know, Capon's lawyers are working overtime to keep him out of prison. The Treasury Department attorneys have him nailed for not filing income tax returns over the past six years." He smiled and winked.

Johnny Sparrowski shook his head and smiled, too.

Elliot Nest turned to leave. Stopping at the door, he said, "Looks like Capon is going up the river for a long time, Johnny. He'll be spending time with all his jailbird friends...!"

Fairest of Them All

As the winter sun set in a crimson blaze to the west, a near full moon crept over the snowcapped mountains to the east, casting its variegated hues of silver and blue over the landscape.

Dhumbo Thumass, the Royal Gatesperson, signaled for the closing of the inner gate and the lifting of the drawbridge.

With loud clanking of heavy chains, the massive bridge was lifted from its footing across the deep moat, and with creaking groans lifted and slammed into the seat near the top of the twin towers.

The sentinel watching from atop the eastern turret sounded a lonely toll of the castle's chapel bells. Everything was secured for the night.

⁂

Dyther Jhaybyrd, Clown Prince of Idyott Castle, climbed the stone stairs to the upper levels, slipping into the topmost and darkest chamber.

As his eyes became accustomed to the darkness, he fixed them on the Magic Mirror in its gilt frame, surface smooth but opaque and darker than the whispering woods during the winter's new moon.

Jhaybyrd approached the mirror, eyes wide and unblinking. Gently he touched the unreflecting surface. It felt cold to the touch and without life.

He hesitated, uncertain whether he wanted truly to ask his question again; not sure he wanted to argue his case with the Seer of the Silvered Window.

"Damn!" he cursed half to himself, "Damn! Damn! Damn…!" He looked out of the corner of his eye, a sideways glance.

Then, gathering himself, he stood full in front of the ornate mirror, and fixing his amber-green eyes on the center of the dark expanse asked, "Oh Mighty Mirror, Your Holiness—who is the most beautiful person in all the realm?"

Silence.

The walls of the castle held their breath. Jhaybyrd waited, perspiration forming on his forehead and in the folds of skin at his neck.

Still, silence.

He stepped back, hesitant, irritation building within, and his eyes narrowed almost imperceptibly. Almost.

Again, "Oh Holy Mirror—I beseech you, who is the most beautiful person in all the realm?" The mirror stirred ever so slightly, but still there was only silence.

Jhaybyrd fidgeted, body twitching as he struggled to be patient.

In these matters, one mustn't press too hard.

The mirror stirred yet again. This time a faint light, dingy-grey and icy cold, glowed within the silvered face. It spread across the curved surface of glass and grew, becoming a bright presence in the room, pushing back the darkness, illuminating the darkest and coldest corners.

Jhaybyrd could hardly remain still as the silence continued.

Then came the answer, flashed across the mirror in bold eighteen-point font:

"PrincessDi@CastleTremayne.com."

Jhaybyrd was stunned, angered by the message on the dingy-grey screen.

"Surely you jest?" stammered the Clown Prince, disbelieving. "Princess Diana is a fairy tale once told and already fading. Her beauty is merely skin deep, and it too is passing. And she is married to that upstart frog, Prince UpChuck!" continued Jhaybyrd, his anger now full-blown and unbridled. "How can that be a consideration in matters of position, let alone beauty?" The prince scowled and stamped his feet before pacing to and fro.

The Holy Mirror stirred and shook, lights flashing across the curved glass surface. Then, in a window at the center of the mirror, it announced in blood-chilling words:

"General Protection Fault: You have completed an illegal procedure. If you elect to continue, your Holy Mirror will exit to the initial prompt, and you will lose all previously unsaved work...!"

Jhaybyrd looked with unbelieving eyes at the steel-grey surface.

"Damn!" he cried. "Damn TinySoft...!"

As he watched, the steel-grey light dimmed and the glass went blank, pitch black in fact, with only the See Prompt in the upper left corner remaining.

Jhaybyrd started to boot the mirror across the room but stayed his anger. "I shall reboot again on the morrow," he muttered under his breath, removing his finger from the reset button.

Dyther Jhaybyrd stormed out of the darkened room and retreated down the spiral stairs from the dark tower.

🦢   🦢   🦢

"Dumoxx!" he screamed, his eyes filled with rage. "Dumoxx! Come at once to the royal chambers! The damned Holy Mirror has crashed again!"

Dumoxx Jhimbo, Consultant to the Clown Prince and Chancellor of Soft Wear, came stumbling into the royal chambers.

"I have a soft wear problem," bellowed Jhaybyrd, "now fix it!"

Jhimbo recoiled at the vehemence of Jhaybyrd's outburst, and rolling his eyes mumbled half to himself, "At once, your Clownness."

Jhimbo went to the royal closet and, sliding the doors open wide, surveyed the Clown Prince's wealth of fine clothing.

"Your memory is insufficient," muttered Jhimbo, this time more to himself than the king. "The Holy Mirror's message is always the same."

"What's that you say?" roared the Clown Prince from the other room. "What are you muttering about?"

"Nothing, your Clownness," whimpered Jhimbo. "It's just that—we upgraded your whole wardrobe, and not that long ago!"

"You said the tailor digitally re-mastered those garments!" roared the Clown Prince. "You told me we wouldn't have to download all that clothing to the less fortunate until the next fashion season!"

"That I did, your Clownness," stammered Jhimbo, feeling increasingly ill at ease. "But—but, bugs just have a way of getting into soft wear—that's the way it is with digitally made clothing, your Clownness."

He was very careful with what he said to the prince in moments like this, for he disliked being the one to remind him of his failing memory. The Clown Prince took his memory problems very seriously.

Jhimbo sighed and pulled a silk cape with ermine trappings from the rack, holding it up to the light coming in the high window.

"Damned bugs!" whispered Jhimbo beneath his breath.

He shook the cape, and several tiny creeping things dropped to the floor, crawling toward the dark corners of the room.

"Hmmm," said Jhimbo. He turned as the door to the royal bedroom opened behind him.

Dhumbo Thumass entered, joining Jhimbo in the royal bedchambers. As the formal Gatesperson, it was Thumass's responsibility to ensure that all the Clown Prince's royal clothing was bundled together for convenience and ease of hanging in the royal closets.

Jhimbo, though, was troubled that everything came all tied together, for it meant more work for him in upgrading the Clown Prince's wardrobe if he had to separate everything before hanging each article of clothing. He much preferred hanging individual articles with separate system hookups.

Thumass, though, cunningly exerted his powerful mind-numbing influence on the Clown Prince, and so the bundling continued.

Dyther Jhaybyrd had primped and fussed with his appearance since his youth. He was obsessed with his looks, and preoccupied with his reputation as the most beautiful of all people.

Dhumbo Thumass had been drawn to him because he, too, was obsessed with the most beautiful of people, though personally he was preoccupied more with their wealth. It was in the wallets of the beautiful and wealthy that Thumass sought his fortunes.

Dumoxx Jhimbo was brought to Idyott Castle because of his reputation as a wardrobe consultant and master of soft wear. Now he was faced with upgrading the Clown Prince's entire wardrobe for a re-visitation to the Magic Mirror. His own reputation counted on his success, as did his ongoing health and well-being.

He and Thumass took various articles of clothing from the closet and shook each fervently, shaking loose a number of tiny bugs. There was something very satisfying in this.

Jhaybyrd silently entered the dressing room and surveyed the work of his trusty aides. He frowned, motioning quickly with his hands, and Jhimbo held up a regal high-end cape with leopard collar and ermine fringes. The Clown Prince slipped his arms into the sleeves.

Jhimbo fastened the silver clasp at the Clown Prince's neck and stepped back.

The Clown Prince looked over his shoulder at himself in the full-length mirror and beheld a magnificently appointed profile, clothed with impressive heavy fabrics of rich amber hues. The bejeweled gold crown on his head capped a most dashing and fashionable royal figure.

Jhaybyrd was most pleased; Jhimbo himself beamed; and Thumass smirked, eyelids half-closed.

✥　✥　✥

Jhaybyrd strode up the spiral stairs once again, his flowing cape trailing behind, reaching the dark upper chamber in short order. He held his head high and stepped into the dark room with a renewed sense of importance about himself.

He positioned himself in front of the Holy Mirror, and without hesitation spoke: "Oh Holy Mirror—now, who is the most beautiful person in all the realm?"

Silence.

Jhaybyrd smiled, his eyes mere slits, and settled back so as not to appear pushy, waiting.

Silence.

I can wait you out, thought Jhaybyrd to himself, and he smirked broadly.

Silence.

The walls, responding to the absence of sound, now moved and began to close in on Jhaybyrd. That unsettling feeling he once had returned.

Deafening silence.

"Hmmm...!" This a murmured whisper.

Then, "Dumoxx!" shouted Jhaybyrd, turning from the mirror. "Come at once...!"

Silence.

Then, a clatter of footsteps on stone stairs, and heavy panting; a stumbled step, muffled sounds, a curse; then more footsteps.

Dumoxx stumbled into the dark chamber, breathing deeply, gasping for air.

"Dumoxx...the Holy Mirror won't boot up," whispered the Clown Prince, his shoulders bent and eyes closed, one hand holding his forehead.

Jhimbo could barely see in the darkness, but knew the look of pain on his Clownness's face.

"I am here," said the soft wear expert softly. "Here, let me look."

Jhimbo stepped by the shaken Clown Prince and checked that the cords were still plugged into the back of the mirror; they were.

Jhimbo slid his fingers over the Off/On switch, clicking back and forth—it was working. He checked the surge protector—it was functioning, and the power was still on for the Gilded Window.

Jhimbo's fingers flew over the keyboard, entering a series of commands to the mirror's Dormant Operating System.

Jhaybyrd watched in fascination, marveling at the skill of his Chancellor of Soft Wear.

I must see that he gets a raise at his next performance evaluation, he thought to himself. Then, *Nahh...!*

Jhimbo frowned, puzzled; the mirror wasn't responding.

"Damn! This is going to be tougher than I thought," he muttered.

He was afraid the Clown Prince might have been right when he said the mirror crashed.

Then, too, the Clown Prince may have hit the delete key, erasing something from the hard drive. That wouldn't be too difficult for the Clown Prince to do. In either case, it would be complicated getting the message off the mirror's drive and on-screen again.

But then, even though the message may not have been saved, he knew the contents anyway. In his judgment, the Holy Mirror was right on—Princess Diana was, surely, the most beautiful person in all the realm. Her beauty was not only legendary and timeless; it was more than outward beauty, for she was most beautiful on the inside.

She placed herself with the common people, and walked amongst them as one of them.

She reached out and touched those whom the world rejected— those whom the world cast off and despised for reminding it of their existence.

She embraced the unholy as holy, and gave from the fullness of her heart, making all lives the richer for it.

Oh, she was, indeed, the most beautiful person in all the realm, but Jhimbo knew he could not tell that to the Clown Prince. It would be suicide.

"Damn," said Jhimbo again. He tapped the keys with yet another command, and the dark curved glass surface shuddered; then there was the familiar whirring as the soft wear responded and took his commands, the dingy-grey light of the mirror appearing once more.

Jhimbo entered several more commands, these designed to tickle out the lost message.

The lights in the mirror brightened, and the See Prompt

appeared in the upper left corner. Jhimbo typed in "win," hit the "Enter" key and waited.

The mirror filled with magical colors and shapes, and the inner workings of the Golden Oval Glass could be heard in the dark room.

He inserted his special soft wear–enhancing disk to heighten the appearance of royal clothing as it appeared in the mirror, typed in "run" and when asked hit "OK," then waited again.

Jhaybyrd watched as his soft wear expert worked his magic, as shapes and colors gave way to spectacular visions of the world of Princess Diana. And in a clear voice-over, the mirror whispered,

"PrincessDi@CastleTremayne.com."

"Now, print a damned hard copy...!"

There was a deep bloodcurdling scream, piercing and pained—and it carried into the ether above and beyond the ramparts of Idyott Castle.

Dyther Jhaybyrd fell into a chronically depressed state, and never consulted the Holy Mirror in the dark upper chamber ever again, though he dressed in his finest and often stood in front of his full-length wardrobe mirror for hours mumbling to himself.

He fired Dumoxx Jhimbo, his Chancellor of Soft Wear, who left Idyott Castle and sought a position elsewhere with a kingdom developing something called a MaqIntosh. With that move the Clown Prince ensured his self-destruction, as his wonderfully artic-ulated clothing withered and deteriorated into utter disarray. It is said the problem with bugs increased a thousand-fold, driving Jhaybyrd to total distraction and madness...

As for Dhumbo Thumass, he also left the company of the Clown

Prince, seeking a position elsewhere as Gatesperson to further research and develop his money-making soft wear and wardrobe packaging systems...

—With apologies to Uncle Walt—and all due respect to lovely Princess Diana, in another age and another time...

The Flute Maker and the Song of the Buffalo

Shadows crept across the mesa overlooking the Valley of the Dunes as the sun passed low over the endless desert, nestling momentarily in the crook of the Whispering Mountains before slipping behind the distant ridges.

Brave Turtle watched in silence as the skies over the western horizon gradually shifted from the amber of eventide through shades of lavender to deep violet, and then into the pitch darkness of the realms of night.

The ancient though familiar travelers of the night sky peeked through the growing canopy of darkness, marking their ageless pathways across the heavens.

The tiny points of light touched memory traces deep in the recesses of Brave Turtle's mind. In deep contentment he sat under the night skies and listened to the song of the Ancients as it wafted across the heavens and whispered through the trees in the canyons below.

❧   ❧   ❧

Hannah slipped off the seat of the buckboard and onto the dusty trail that led through the valley in the direction of the Canyon of the Ancients.

Uncle Terry held the horses steady as Hannah waved goodbye and made her way down the trail and into the underbrush.

"You be careful, y'hear?" yelled Uncle Terry after her.

"I will," replied Hannah.

"And you call when you get to Grandma Ann's," added Uncle Terry.

"OK, don't worry." And then she was gone.

The sun was past midday and still threatening to raise temperatures, but there was a light cloud cover to take the edge off the heat. Hannah was traveling light but was prepared for anything.

She knew that a sudden storm could come up without warning in the badlands, and if it did the canyons would become raging torrents.

Her plan was to make it through the Valley of the Dunes by nightfall, and bed down under the stars on the bluff above the bend in the river.

Then, with good weather she should make it to the Canyon of the Ancients by late afternoon tomorrow.

Dad would be waiting there, and they would make the final leg of the trip to Grandma Ann's the following day. Hannah adjusted the collar of her windbreaker and set her face for the far mountains.

⋰   ⋰   ⋰

Brave Turtle took the hand of the young girl walking with him, and as they ambled beneath the trees in the silent canyon, he told her the story of the Flute Maker of the Ancients.

"He walked amongst these very trees and spoke with the buffalo from the great plains," said Brave Turtle. "He listened to the beating of their hearts, and to their taking in of the breath that gives life. He listened to their dreams and their longings, listened as they told their offspring tales told by the Ancients to their offspring in ages long gone by. He listened to the wind coming off the prairie that tells the buffalo of a coming thunderstorm."

The young girl looked into the steel-grey eyes of her elder, expression lighting up as a smile crossed her lips.

"Did he really listen to the buffalo, Brave Turtle?" asked the young girl.

"The Flute Maker was a very wise man, and he knew many languages, but he was a most skilled listener," said Brave Turtle. "He, above all others, heard the song of the buffalo."

Hannah found the going was getting more difficult because the path wasn't clearly marked. She tried to stay on the shortest most direct route through the valley, but occasionally found that she had to go around a rock formation or an impenetrable stand of shrubs. Going over a rock barrier was the most difficult, and the most tiring.

She checked her compass against her topo-map several times to make sure she was moving in the right direction, and she thought she was.

The sun seemed to move quickly over the arc of the afternoon. Approaching the riverbend, she could feel the wind kick up a little.

It was a dry wind, and warm, gently rustling the leaves of the cottonwoods near the river's edge.

She climbed a slight rise to the bluff above the river and picked out a flat area near the edge overlooking the valley.

Tired, she lay in the open under the stars and dropped off to sleep.

⇟ ⇟ ⇟

Hannah was up before the sun, and after a quick breakfast of power bars set off in the direction of the Canyon of the Ancients.

She came to two huge rocks barring her way and started down the narrow gap between them. As she neared the bottom she slipped on a rock and went tumbling headlong onto the dirt landing below.

She felt a little dizzy and, thinking she might have suffered a bump when she fell, shook her head to clear it.

"Are you hurt, little one?" came a soft voice from behind her.

Startled, she swung around and found herself looking into the face of an old man—a face of timeworn wrinkles and dark skin, topped by a shock of silver-grey hair.

His eyes were large, steel-grey and deep, yet kind and warm.

A young girl stood at his side, and her large brown eyes looked out of a face framed in hair of jet black.

"Who are you?" Hannah stammered, her voice wavering.

"Are you hurt?" asked steel-grey eyes again.

"Hunuuh," replied Hannah cautiously.

The elder man knelt beside her. "I am Brave Turtle, and my young companion is called by the name Talon of the Eagle."

"Are you able to get up and walk?" asked the young girl.

"Yes, I think so," answered Hannah, and she gingerly rose to her feet. She was unsteady but remained standing.

"What are you doing in the Valley of the Dunes without an elder?" asked Brave Turtle. "Are you lost?"

"No, I know where I am, and I'm twelve and can take care of myself," responded Hannah, a little irritated. "I'm on my way to my grandmother's house on the other side of the Canyon of the Ancients."

"Ah, you know of the Ancients?" asked Brave Turtle, his eyes suddenly alight.

The young girl stood silently beside him, her eyes, too, fixed on Hannah.

"Well, I only know stories my father used to tell me." Hannah was hesitant, searching the closets of her memory.

"He used to tell me bedtime stories that he said were about the Ancient People from around here. There was this wise old man—a storyteller—who told of a Flute Maker that walked with the buffalo and talked with them."

At this the young girl smiled, her eyes growing large.

Brave Turtle nodded.

"Yes—it seems your father knows well the stories of my people."

Hannah's eyes narrowed ever so slightly. "What do you mean my father knows about your people?" she asked.

Brave Turtle was silent for a moment.

"The man of whom your father spoke knew the Flute Maker," said Brave Turtle with a smile. "The ancient artist would visit the River of Sighs and, searching amongst the trees, find just the right slender branch for his instrument. He was very careful in selecting the right wood, listening for its song, and would sometimes take a full cycle of the moon to find the right one."

Hannah held Brave Turtle's eyes.

"The Flute Maker would take that twig and work the wood just so, and in his nimble hands the wood came to life and in concert worked with him, and it became the finest of vessels for the songs of the Ancients."

Brave Turtle paused, and as he did so Hannah whispered, "This is the same story my father told me when I was younger."

Brave Turtle nodded and continued, "By the next new moon, the buffalo heard a deep music, as though the heart of the night sky itself sounded—low, almost below a warrior's hearing, it would beat as their hearts beat."

Brave Turtle pointed beyond the treetops to the ridge of the canyon above them.

"Do you see the high point in the rocks above? It is the place where the sun first strikes the earth in the morning—a place where the sun at twilight last touches the earth before making its nightward journey."

As Brave Turtle paused again, Hannah added, "The Flute Maker would stand in that spot and his music would rise to the heavens, and the buffalo would weep."

"Yes," answered Brave Turtle, nodding. Then his eyes grew dark and took on a pall, as though a shadow had passed over them.

"Sadly, the Ancients were visited by men of darkness—those who dwelled in the shadows for their strength, who delighted in the misfortunes of others. Theirs was not a path chosen for its light, but for ill deeds of a darker more sinister nature."

Brave Turtle sighed. "Toal Hellsohn was the most vicious and unfeeling. Given to attacks against great and small alike, he held forth with such intense ferocity as to kill the spirit of the people.

"Jason Guylland was the most eloquent of these men, speaking in the silvered tongues of the Ancients. A most deceptive skill, for he spoke with a split tongue, and his ill thoughts turned the people from the sun until they saw naught but shadows in their midst, the very handmaidens of evil."

The old man now bowed his head. "Their hearts hardened, and life became spare and without hope—the breath of life had left them."

Hannah struggled to understand as Brave Turtle went on: "But one Jamison Brushton was the coldest of these three, and blood ran cold at the mere mention of his name. His eyes were deep pools of anger, unfathomable in their darkness, and cold as places in the deepest heavens hid from the ancient lights. These men freely dispensed their collective venom, poisoning the land, the hearts, and the souls of the people. Life among the people could not be sustained, and in time they died away, most of a broken spirit."

The young girl was saddened on hearing this story—the Ancients were a people of mystery, proud and full of life, and she had up to this time heard nothing but their stories of living and creation. Saddened by this revelation, her eyes filled until huge tears rolled down her cheeks.

Hannah reached out a hand and laid it gently on her arm. and taking her by the shoulders pulled her into herself and held her.

Brave Turtle, his eyes shining with a deep fire, reached out his arms and enveloped the two young girls in his large and warm embrace.

"Do not weep, young one," he whispered. "The Flute Maker is alive still, and his ancient art prevails—his song comes on the south winds that glean from the prairies the song of the buffalo. You hear his song in the dew of the morn that graces the flowers of the hillsides. It is in the scent of newly turned earth, and in the call of the raven echoing from the deepest canyons. It is in the eyes of all creatures, and in your own heart, if you but remember. So, be still and know that the song of the buffalo is still heard and not forgotten."

Hannah blinked her eyes, and again shook her head—it still hurt a little. She found herself lying at the base of the narrow gap between the two huge rock formations she was climbing down when she fell.

The earth was soft, cushioned by a layering of grasses and low-lying shrubs that broke her fall.

She sat up and felt her arms and legs. Scratched up a bit, though she seemed intact and nothing felt broken. Hannah looked around but found herself alone.

"Hello...! Anyone there? Brave Turtle...!" she called out, her voice lost in the trees above her. Silence—not even the gentle whisper of the wind in the cottonwoods nearby.

Hannah dusted herself off, all the while looking around to find her companions.

Nothing.

She checked her watch—4:35—time she was on her way if she meant to reach the rim of the Canyon of the Ancients by nightfall.

⌇   ⌇   ⌇

The sun completed its arc across the heavens, its light arriving at the rim of the canyon at the same time as Hannah—at dusk.

The light cloud cover had cleared, leaving the skies a deep azure. As the sun set beyond the western ridges, the heavens underwent their nightly transformation from the realm of the sun to the realm of night, and Hannah could feel the earth making its peaceful transformation.

As she approached the grand oak tree just back from the rim of the canyon, she heard her name called.

"Hannah—hey, Hon—over here."

Dad stood leaning against the ancient guardian of the canyon, a smile lighting his face.

Hannah waved and rushed over to him, throwing her arms around his neck.

"Hey, what's with this?" blurted her father, "Are you OK...?"

"Yeah, I'm all right," answered Hannah, "but, do I have something to tell you...!"

Appendix

Postscript

There is a history behind the selection of short stories contained in *Meanderings of a Bent Mind*. It involves an intense situation at my work for a social service agency in the late 1980s and early 1990s.

I loved working with my clients knowing I was providing much-needed services and support to them and their families. There was a period early on when I came under severe stress because of abusive treatment by management personnel. This was a situation all staff experienced, so I wasn't in it alone. For a brief time I considered leaving the agency, but as I loved my work with my clients I chose to remain and sought some alternative remedy to ease the stress. I was under no illusions I could change the abusive people.

As a trained social worker, I was cognizant of the consequences of stress not addressed and considered the possibility of seeking therapy to help myself. After some thought I turned instead to three artistic avenues as a non-chemical means of self-medication: photography, the art of embroidery, and creative writing.

My wife was most understanding and gave consent for me to purchase camera gear, and I ended up with high-quality professional photographic equipment. Early on I attended numerous photography workshops to hone my skill behind the camera. I found the process serene, relaxing, and healing, while I learned how to see the world around me. The benefit came as the beginnings of a remedy to the stress I was experiencing at work.

The second avenue I pursued to relieve stress was the needlework of embroidery. Rather than using stock designs that came with embroidery kits, I elected to create my own patterns to work with needle and thread. My initial project was a very complex and detailed Samurai warrior taken from a Japanese children's coloring book. As with my photographic efforts, I found this relaxing, soothing, and peaceful.

The third method was a turn at creative writing. I had always thought of myself as a writer, though truth be told much of what came through my pen wasn't of a quality to make any fuss over. Here's the thing, though—I really enjoyed the writing.

I set for myself the task of writing short stories, generally in three to four typed pages, with a beginning, middle, and an ending. Some extended to seven to eight pages. My stories usually involved a protagonist, often a young girl of ten to twelve, who with the guidance of a mystery muse, a woman of magic, carried the battle against the forces of evil. The villains I cast as the abusive supervisors at my work, and the forces of light always won out over the forces of darkness.

Like the photography and embroidery, the writing served to ease the stress I was experiencing and gave me the satisfaction of battering the abusers as I saved myself. Bottom line, it all worked.

During a three-year period I wrote forty-one short stories, including the twenty-four contained in *Meanderings of a Bent Mind.*

Acknowledgments

My journey as an introvert began with the return of my family from the concentration camp in Colorado just before the end of World War II. It was February 1945, just after the government had relaxed Executive Order 9066 and allowed internees to leave camp and return to their homes.

We arrived in the middle of the school year and before the war in Europe and with Japan had ended, so as I entered Miss Peck's first grade, being somewhat aware as a child, I knew I was not like the other kids.

Over the course of the next several years I noticed what I thought were teachers playing favorites with the white kids when the teacher asked a question of the class—they always picked a white child to answer. I resented this, and held some not nice thoughts about what I was seeing.

Then something shifted: It occurred to me that teachers weren't choosing a white child, they were picking the outgoing child whose hand flew up over the non-outgoing child.

The next time our teacher asked a question I tested my theory, and my hand shot up high. The teacher chose me, and luckily, I knew the answer. I tried this several more times with the same result—I had been wrong. Teachers weren't picking children based on race, they were choosing the outgoing child who enthusiastically raised their hand. I later learned the outgoing child was considered an extrovert, and the non-outgoing child was likely an introvert. I was one of the latter.

In considering this inner journey I began back then, I wish to acknowledge those who helped show the way for me to develop an internal world of magic and mystery, the life of an introvert.

First was Mrs. Ruth Coulson, Mitchell Elementary School, Atwater, California, grade seven. After lunch each day, she did something special: We'd rest our heads on our desks, close our eyes, and she would read to us for thirty minutes from one of her favorite books. She asked us in our mind's eye to imagine what we heard using all our senses—what were we seeing, could we taste something, did we feel the warmth of its touch, what did we hear, and what were we feeling? This opened a whole new world of imagination and sped me on my inner travels.

Another person who contributed to this passage was Mr. Jones, Livingston High School, Livingston, California, Latin I and Latin II. At the beginning of the first semester Mr. Jones introduced himself as a teacher of a dead language, Latin. However, he promised we were going to bring this language back to life by not just translating word for word into English, but with the aid of our many senses giving each word a life of its own. Like Mrs. Coulson, Mr. Jones invited us into an inner realm where magic and wonder are found.

Lastly, I wish to acknowledge my father, Ben Noriaki Nagai, a Japanese immigrant alien who came to the United States in 1917 as a thirteen-year-old. He spent several years in school near San Jose, California, just long enough to learn a little English, then left to find work, helping support his family.

He married my mother in 1931, and together they bought a farm and settled down to raise a family. He was a quiet man who had little to say most of the time, partly because (as I learned later) he was an introvert, but also because his English was weak, and thus he most often chose silence.

My relationship with my dad was hard because he didn't speak very much. When I asked a question, he had single-word answers or shrugged his shoulders. I soon learned not to ask, and instead just watched.

A lot went on internally and unsaid, and it was difficult for me to decipher what was going on with him. Though I didn't know it at the time, I did learn a lot just from his non-verbal non-action actions. I became very much like him, with a solid work ethic, a sense of right and wrong, a valuing of family, and the disposition for treating people right.

Thus, on this journey of an introvert, and in the end and out of it all, I am my father's son.

Gordon's Bio

Gordon Hideaki Nagai is a second-generation American of Japanese ancestry. He was the eldest son to a second-generation Japanese American mother and a first-generation Japanese father and grew up on a farm just outside the town of Atwater, California. He and his family were forcibly evacuated during World War II to a concentration camp in Colorado, where they lived for three years surrounded by barbed wire fences and guard towers. They returned to their family-owned farm in early February 1945 before war's end.

He attended elementary school in Atwater and high school in Livingston in central San Joaquin Valley, California. He then graduated from the University of California at Berkeley with a Master of Social Welfare degree.

He served two years of alternative service as a conscientious objector in lieu of military service with the California Department of Mental Hygiene, then thirty-five years as a social worker for several social service agencies. In the late '60s and early '70s he was active in the Civil Rights movement and protesting the war in Vietnam.

Gordon's recent literary work is a memoir-style novel he collaborated in writing with a friend from high school, titled *Two Faces*. It tells of two ten-year-old friends, a white girl and a Japanese boy, whose lives are disrupted by the bombing of Pearl Harbor, and how they face and deal with racial prejudice that follows.

Gordon has also self-published eight booklets of puns, a volume from the perspective of an introvert punster addressing how he thinks, and *The Ultimate Book of Dad Jokes* and *Born to Pun*, both published by Ulysses Press, Berkeley, CA. All are available through local bookstores and on Amazon.com.

You may read more at Gordon's blog:
https://journeysofabentmind.wordpress.com

9 781965 278758